Ben stood by the front door, wondering if turning up unannounced was the right thing to do.

His thought processes hadn't been that clear for the past four or five days. Since he'd last spoken to Maggie. Since she'd dropped her bombshell.

The door opened.

'Ben!' She stepped straight into his arms.

He'd been planning on keeping his distance when he got here, physically as well as emotionally, but what could he do? Feeling her against his chest, it was a natural reflex to wrap his arms around her and hold her tight. Hugging her felt right. But it shouldn't. It couldn't. He dropped his arms and stepped back.

'We need to talk. And it isn't a conversation I thought we could have over the phone.' Nothing was making sense. Seeing Maggie again, feeling her touch, hearing her voice, was confusing him. He remembered how he'd missed her. Missed the softness of her skin, the smell of her hair.

He remembered the plans that had been forming in his mind when he left. Plans for him and Maggie. But those plans had centred around the two of them. Not around the two of them…and children.

Emily Forbes is the pseudonym of two sisters who share both a passion for writing and a life-long love of reading. Beyond books and their families, their interests include cooking (food is a recurring theme in their books!), learning languages, playing the piano and netball, as well as an addiction to travel—armchair is fine, but anything involving a plane ticket is better. Home for both is South Australia, where they live three minutes apart with their husbands and four young children. With backgrounds in business administration, law, arts, clinical psychology and physiotherapy, they have worked in many areas. This past professional experience adds to their writing in many ways: legal dilemmas, psychological ordeals and business scandals are all intermeshed with the medical settings of their stories. And, since nothing could ever be as delicious as spending their days telling the stories of gorgeous heroes and spirited heroines, they are eternally grateful their mutual dream of writing for a living came true.

They would love you to visit and keep up to date with current news and future releases at the Medical™ Romance authors' website: http://medicalromance.blogspot.com

Recent titles by the same author:

THE PLAYBOY FIREFIGHTER'S PROPOSAL
WEDDING AT PELICAN BEACH
THE SURGEON'S LONGED-FOR BRIDE

DR DROP-DEAD GORGEOUS

BY
EMILY FORBES

First published in Great Britain 2010
Large Print edition 2011
Harlequin Mills & Boon Limited,
Eton House, 18-24 Paradise Road,
Richmond, Surrey TW9 1SR

© Emily Forbes 2010

ISBN: 978 0 263 21711 7

Printed and bound in Great Britain
by CPI Antony Rowe, Chippenham, Wiltshire

DR DROP-DEAD GORGEOUS

To my very own Drop-Dead Gorgeous husband and romantic inspiration, James, and our two gorgeous boys, Ned & Finn— it is the most amazing feeling to have your support and to know how proud you are of my writing. You are the most precious people in the world to me and this book is for you with my thanks and love.

CHAPTER ONE

'JULIET! Can you hear me? Stay with us, Juliet.'

Maggie woke with a start. She was in strange surroundings, curled up and cramped in an armchair. She rubbed her neck with one hand as she tried to work out where she was. The room came into focus. A drip stand, an overway table, white sheets on a single bed—a hospital room.

She remembered where she was. She was waiting for her sister to come out of Theatre.

She looked around, searching for the person whose voice had woken her. A man's voice, she was sure of it. He'd been talking loudly but the room was quiet now; she was alone.

Had she been dreaming?

Her heart was thumping in her chest—she put her hand over it, as if she could slow it down. She had been dreaming; she could recall it now. She'd been dreaming about Juliet's operation.

Juliet's heart had stopped and the doctors had been using cardiac paddles to get it going again. That was what had woken her so abruptly. That was why her heart was racing—it was as though she'd felt the shock of the charge going through her own chest.

Something had gone wrong and she needed to find out what it was.

She jumped out of the chair.

How long had she been sleeping? She checked her watch, quarter past two. Juliet should have been out of Theatre by now. Someone must know something.

Maggie needed information; she needed to know what had happened and she needed to know if Juliet was OK.

She made her way to the nurses' station. The nurse sitting at the desk was the one who'd come to take Juliet to Theatre. Maggie was relieved there hadn't been a change of shift yet. She had no time for pleasantries or to explain who she was.

'Carol, do you know if Juliet is out of Theatre yet?'

The nurse looked up and must have recognised her. 'I haven't heard anything. Would you like me to check?'

'Please. I thought she'd be finished by now.' Maggie tapped her foot impatiently.

Carol picked up the phone and punched in the extension number, frowning as the call went unanswered. 'There's no answer but if they're busy they don't always pick up.'

Maggie knew that was true but she immediately wondered what was happening in Theatre or Recovery that would make the phone go unanswered. Was Juliet all right?

'I'll try again in a minute and come and find you. Will you wait in Juliet's room?' Carol waited for Maggie to nod before returning her attention to her paperwork.

Maggie made a pretence of returning to her sister's room but there was no way she'd be able to sit and wait. She walked past the door and headed for the lift to take her up to Theatres and Recovery.

She paced around the confines of the lift as it carried her to the top floor. She exited the lift and followed the signs, hurrying along the corridor to the recovery suites and pressing the call button by the door. She pressed it twice before a nurse responded.

Maggie barely waited for the nurse to ask what she wanted before she spoke. 'I'm Juliet Taylor's sister. Can you tell me how she is?'

The nurse's eyes widened and Maggie's eyes narrowed in response as she tried to work out what was bothering the girl. Was she surprised to find a stranger hovering by the door or was she trying to formulate an answer? Maggie suspected that something had happened and that this nurse didn't want to be the one to tell her about it.

'What happened? Is she OK?'

The nurse continued to stand there, mute.

Maggie recognised the nurse's expression now. Something unexpected had happened in Theatre and Maggie had been right to come barging up here to find out what. Something had happened to Juliet.

There was a flurry of movement behind the nurse. Maggie peered over her shoulder and saw a patient being wheeled into Recovery. She shoved her foot in the doorway to prevent the nurse from closing her out and waited, trying to catch a glimpse of the patient on the barouche. Was it Juliet? She couldn't relax until she saw her sister with her own eyes.

There was quite a crowd surrounding the bed, fussing about as they connected the patient to various monitors. It was difficult to see who was lying there but as the nurse backed away Maggie had a strong suspicion the patient was Juliet. She wasn't waiting any longer—somebody must be able to tell her something. She looked around for someone, anyone, who didn't appear to be busy.

She saw the nurse she'd spoken to approach one of the other theatre staff—a man—and saw her point at the doorway, at Maggie. Maggie focused on her as she directed her comment to the room in general.

'Excuse me, I'm Juliet Taylor's sister. Could someone please tell me what's going on?'

The man looked in her direction, issued what seemed to be instructions to the other staff and started towards her.

There was no hesitation on his part. He walked confidently. He looked as if he was used to being in control; he looked like a man who could avert a disaster.

Something in his walk told Maggie that even if there had been a problem, he'd solved it. He didn't walk like a man who was about to deliver bad news. Maggie felt herself relax; she could breathe normally again.

'You're Juliet's sister?'

Maggie nodded. 'I'm Maggie Petersen.'

'Ben McMahon, Juliet's plastic surgeon.' He held out his hand, offering to shake hers. His grip was warm and strong. Comforting, Maggie thought as she put her hand in his and felt her heart stop its crazy hammering and return to its normal rhythm, calmed by this man's touch.

'Is she OK?'

'Yes, she's going to be fine but there were some complications.'

'What sort of complications?' Maggie's heart skipped a beat and she took a deep breath, willing herself to stay calm, willing her heart to beat normally. Juliet had cheated death once before—could she be lucky a second time?

'Let's find somewhere to sit down.' He led her around a corner to a room with several recliner chairs lining the walls. It was obviously used for day-surgery patients but at the moment it was vacant.

Ben waited for her to sit in one recliner, then he sat on the edge of the next one facing her. It looked as though he was trying to work out how to phrase his words gently and Maggie didn't have the patience for that. 'I'm a nurse—just tell me what happened.'

He jerked back a little, perhaps surprised by her abruptness, but he recovered quickly and answered Maggie's question without hesitating. 'Juliet's reconstructive surgery went well—I was pleased with that aspect—but as the anaesthetist was about to reverse the anaesthetic Juliet's blood pressure plummeted. You saw her in recovery—' he waited for Maggie to nod in assent '—so you know she's pulled through but her heart did stop and we had to resuscitate her.'

Maggie recalled her dream—maybe it hadn't been as strange as it seemed. Her voice was tight as she forced her next question out. 'She's fine now?'

'We'll keep a close eye on her, of course, but so far she's fine.'

'How long did it take to revive her?' Maggie needed facts.

'About ninety seconds.'

Within safe time limits, Maggie knew. 'What triggered the drop in BP?' she asked.

'The anaesthetist suspects it might have been a reaction to the antinausea drug. That's not uncommon but it's reassuring to know that in patients who've experienced this reaction there have been no long-term after-effects.'

Maggie could hear what Dr McMahon was telling her—Juliet would be fine—but she'd had a sense of unease about this surgery from the beginning and now she wondered what else could go wrong. She hadn't been convinced that Juliet had needed this surgery but it hadn't been her decision and there'd been no way of stopping Juliet once she'd made up her mind. That had been the case their whole lives. Juliet didn't wait for other people to make her decisions. She didn't leave it up to fate either. Juliet did what Juliet wanted and when.

This operation was a perfect example, Maggie

thought. Juliet had been diagnosed with breast cancer twelve months ago. She'd undergone a bilateral mastectomy even though the cancer had been in one breast only. When she found out that, due to a faulty gene, she had a high chance of getting cancer in her other breast she'd very quickly decided to have both removed. Now she had just completed the first step of breast reconstruction. Maggie hadn't seen the point of a reconstruction but, as Juliet had pointed out, it wasn't her body, and Juliet had been adamant that was what she was going to do. And now it had nearly killed her.

Maggie had always thought the surgery unnecessary and now it had almost cost Juliet her life. A life she'd fought so desperately to save just twelve months earlier. Maggie sighed, knowing that even this latest drama wouldn't stop Juliet from going after what she wanted.

'Are you OK?'

Dr McMahon's hand on her arm startled Maggie out of her reverie. She'd forgotten she wasn't alone. She lifted her head. He was looking at her with concern. Worried she was about to collapse too? She was quite OK. The only thing upsetting her equilibrium was Dr McMahon—he was seriously gorgeous and sitting far too close. She just remembered to nod in reply to his question even as she registered that his eyes were the exact same blue as his theatre scrubs.

'Come with me—I'll take you in to see for yourself. She's going to be fine. Trust me.'

And for some reason she couldn't explain, Maggie did trust this man. This man she'd only just met. Somehow she believed if he said everything would be fine, it would be.

She followed him along the corridor, back to Recovery. His back filled her field of vision. He was more than six foot by a couple of inches, Maggie guessed, solidly built, not fat but fit. He filled out his scrubs nicely—broad shoulders, narrower hips with his trousers tied loosely around them. Maggie was well aware just how unflattering theatre clothes could be but somehow, despite this, he managed to pull off the look. Some people would look good in a sack and Maggie suspected this man was one them. He could be a poster boy for tall, dark and handsome men.

Maggie stayed beside her sister, keeping one eye on the monitors that displayed her blood pressure, heart rate and oxygen levels, and one eye on the gentle rise and fall of the sheets as Juliet breathed in and out. Ben had been telling the truth—Juliet seemed fine. There was nothing for Maggie to do except watch. Watch and think. She thought about the past two years, about what Juliet had been through, but she also thought about Dr Ben McMahon. He'd left Recovery after checking on Juliet's status but Maggie could very easily recall his turquoise gaze and his calm and confident aura. She was glad he'd been there; she felt reassured.

She stayed until she was sure Juliet was OK, until she was certain she could go home and tell Juliet's children their mother was fine.

Maggie felt as though she'd barely slept for two nights. She was staying at Juliet's house to look after the children but they were unsettled and missing their mother and Maggie's nerves were stretched. She was tired and stressed, worried about her sister's recovery. Each time she woke during the night she rang the hospital to check on Juliet. Her recovery had been unremarkable and, just as Dr McMahon had predicted, there'd been no more dramas and everything seemed back to normal.

Juliet was expecting to be discharged today. She'd asked Maggie to get to the hospital as early as possible, anticipating going home. She was obviously feeling better—she was certainly pushing to be discharged—but nothing much had ever slowed Juliet down.

Maggie had just managed to get Juliet's children ready and to school on time before she returned to the hospital. She'd showered but hadn't had time to wash her hair. She'd pulled it back into a ponytail and thrown on a pair of old jeans and a jumper but no make-up. She thought she probably looked worse than Juliet.

Juliet had been moved out of HDU into a private room after twenty-four hours but she'd spent most of yesterday sleeping and she looked surprisingly good. I *do* look worse than her, Maggie decided.

She walked over to the bed, leaning over to kiss Juliet's cheek. 'Hi. How are you feeling?'

'A bit tired and sore but otherwise fine, surprisingly enough.'

'Ready to go home, do you think?'

'Definitely. I'm just waiting for the surgeon to come and discharge me.'

That would be Ben. Maggie's heart flip-flopped in her chest. She hadn't seen him yesterday when she'd visited Juliet, but she didn't want to admit she'd felt disappointed. 'Did he explain to you what happened?'

'They think I had a reaction to the antinausea drug but there don't seem to be any ongoing problems and they certainly don't seem to be expecting any,' Juliet replied.

'Do you remember anything? Were you scared?'

Juliet shook her head. 'Not at all. It was the strangest experience though. It was just like I've heard people describe it. The light. That floating sensation. How safe you feel. Everything.' She paused and then continued. 'Steven was there.'

'My Steven?'

Juliet nodded.

'Did you see him?' Maggie didn't doubt her

sister's recollection. Maggie was a theatre nurse; she'd heard plenty of these tales before, too many for her to rule them all out as nonsense.

'No, I couldn't see anything up there. The light was beautiful but it concealed everything. I could look down, I could see the operating theatre, I could see myself—but I couldn't see Steven. I just heard him.'

'What did he say?'

'He told me it wasn't my time. He sent me back. Told me my babies needed me.' Juliet paused. 'Do I sound crazy?'

Maggie shook her head. 'I've had patients tell me similar things before,' she answered honestly. 'Did Steven say anything to me?'

The question was out before she could wonder why she'd even asked it.

What was she hoping to hear? Did she want a message or not? Would it matter either way?

When Steven first passed away Maggie would have given anything for one more chance just to touch him, one more chance to have him hold her, one more chance to hear him whisper her name. But that had been ten years ago and she'd come to terms with her loss. Even though she hadn't found anyone to take Steven's place his absence was no longer a gaping hole in her life—it was just a part of her. A part of her she'd become used to living with.

So why had she asked the question?

Curiosity, she decided. That was the answer.

Juliet shook her head. 'No, sorry, Mags.'

She shrugged; it didn't matter. What had she expected him to say? Only what she imagined she'd want to hear. 'Be happy. I miss you. I love you'?

Did she still love him? She loved him but she couldn't still be *in love* with someone who'd been dead for ten years. That wasn't realistic. It didn't matter that there'd been no message. A message wouldn't change the fact that she was a widow and her life had moved on.

She picked up the chart at the end of the bed and flicked through it, looking for a change in topic. The monitors said Juliet was fine and the charts agreed. The medical staff had checked and double-checked everything and there was nothing untoward going on. Nothing that re-quired further discussion.

'Morning, ladies.'

Maggie looked up from the chart at the sound of Ben's voice. It was rich and deep and she could feel it reverberate through her body. She hurriedly replaced the chart only to realize he was focused on Juliet and apparently not at all concerned about her activities. She silently reprimanded herself for being so foolish. Just because she felt a spark of attraction didn't mean anything. He was obviously just a man doing his job.

'Juliet, how are you?' he asked.

'Great. Packed and ready to go home. Ben, this is my sister, Maggie.'

'Yes, we met.' He glanced in her direction before returning his attention to Juliet. His focus was definitely on his patient, and Maggie swallowed her pride. 'How's your chest?'

'A bit sore but better than yesterday, and otherwise I'm fine.'

Maggie stepped away from the bed, giving Ben space to examine Juliet. She thought putting some distance between them would give her a chance to recover her nerve but all she did was stand there and study him while his attention was focused elsewhere.

His thick dark hair was cut short but it looked as though it would curl if left to grow longer. His jaw was square and firm, perfectly symmetrical. He smiled at something Juliet said and creases appeared in the corners of his eyes. He was leaning over Juliet now, checking her wounds, and his trousers moulded around his buttocks. Maggie felt herself blush and quickly moved her attention a bit higher, away from temptation. From behind him she couldn't see his eyes but she remembered the colour—turquoise blue.

She noticed a few flecks of silver in his hair and guessed him to be in his late thirties or early forties, about her age. The silver did nothing to detract from his looks—he really was gorgeous. But, she supposed, given that he was a plastic surgeon, he *should* be gorgeous. She wondered if he'd had any work done.

He'd finished examining Juliet and was standing in profile now; this allowed Maggie to study his nose, which, for the record, was a perfect

Roman nose, narrow and straight. He turned to face her. 'Is something wrong?'

Had he felt her staring at him? Normally she would have blushed and looked away—normally she would be mortified to have someone catch her staring—but she found herself unable, or unwilling, to break his gaze.

'Your nose.'

Ben reached up, rubbing his nose with one hand as if expecting to find something distasteful there. 'Is that better?' he asked.

'No, no, there wasn't anything wrong with your nose—that was what I was wondering, whether you'd had it fixed.'

'Maggie!' Juliet exclaimed.

'What?' Maggie looked at her sister, relieved to find she was actually able to break Ben's gaze after all.

'You can't ask that.'

'Why not? If I can't ask a plastic surgeon about plastic surgery, who can I ask? Besides, you know I've always hated my nose so if I see a nice nose and I find out it's been surgically assisted I might consider getting my own done.'

'Thank you,' Ben responded. 'I think that

was a compliment, but my nose is one hundred per cent natural, sorry.'

Maggie looked back at him. He was smiling at her, and she immediately forgot what she'd been talking about. If he was gorgeous before, he was now twice as gorgeous. His teeth were perfect, straight and white—what she always thought of as American teeth, the sort all sitcom actors had—but when he smiled she could see a streak of mischief in him that you wouldn't have noticed at first. Not smiling, he was the epitome of a clean-cut, college-educated Aussie male, but when he smiled, she knew he wasn't as wholesome as he first appeared. There was more to him than met the eye—he had a definite larrikin streak, which by no means diminished his appeal. If anything, it made her wonder even more about him. What was he thinking about that could make him smile like that?

His blue eyes sparkled. 'Just out of interest, what's wrong with your nose?'

Maggie touched the bridge of her nose. 'I hate this bump in the middle.'

'That's a hard thing to guarantee to fix, you

know. Think of it as giving you individuality.' Ben delivered his verdict with a wink before turning his attention back to Juliet.

Maggie stood, stuck to the spot as strange sensations flooded through her. This man was disturbing her equilibrium in a major way.

She'd met plenty of attractive, intelligent men in her time but Ben seemed so down-to-earth, with no signs of an overinflated ego. He seemed normal, charming. Or at least he was charming her! But it didn't seem deliberate on his part. It seemed natural. And Maggie was definitely not immune. Her mouth was dry and her hands were shaking; her pulse was racing. She put a hand to her stomach, trying to settle her nerves. Don't be ridiculous, she told herself.

'So, can I go home? Maggie's a nurse—I'll be in good hands.'

Hearing her name brought her attention back to the matter at hand, getting Juliet home. She realized she'd missed most of Ben and Juliet's conversation as she'd tried to get her wayward thoughts under control.

Ben addressed her now. 'That's right—you

told me that the other day, didn't you? What sort of nurse?'

'I work in Theatre.'

'Can you handle patients who are conscious?' Ben's accompanying smile made Maggie's skin tingle. It was the strangest sensation, as if her skin had a life and mind of its own.

'I'll be fine,' she said, smiling back at him, or at least hoping she was smiling and not grinning like a half-crazed woman.

Ben turned his focus back to Juliet. 'In that case I'll discharge you and see you in a fortnight. Have you got your appointment?' Juliet nodded and Ben continued. 'Any concerns, ring me. And remember, no heavy lifting or strenuous housework—that includes shopping for groceries and hanging up washing.'

Both sisters watched him leave the room and once he was supposedly out of earshot Juliet spoke up.

'Told you he was fabulous, didn't I?'

Had she? Maggie couldn't remember. She'd be surprised if Juliet hadn't said something—it wasn't every day you came across someone as striking as Ben—but she could barely remember right now what her own name was let alone whether Juliet had mentioned her handsome plastic surgeon. Silently she did agree that he seemed fabulous but she wasn't sure whether her mind was really processing things properly so she chose to keep her own counsel.

'Pity he's my specialist,' Juliet continued talking, apparently unaware that Maggie hadn't answered her.

'You wouldn't!' Maggie gasped.

'Wouldn't what? Jump into bed with him if I got the chance?' Juliet laughed. ''Course I would. I'm divorced, not dead. I've survived twice now, first breast cancer and then being brought back from death's door two days ago, and I intend to make the most of being alive. Just wait until I get my new boobs—there's more life in this old girl and I intend to enjoy some of it.'

Maggie laughed but also wondered what Juliet would say if she told her that was exactly how she felt!

Her first response hadn't been wrong—Ben was seriously attractive, and she definitely wasn't immune to his physical qualities. The small space of Juliet's hospital room hadn't been able to contain his energy and charisma, and Maggie was just as aware of his appeal today as she had been two days earlier. But, while she could appreciate Ben's attributes, unlike Juliet, she couldn't imagine being with him any more than she was sure he could imagine being with her.

As much as she'd consider the idea in theory she couldn't imagine it ever eventuating in real life. What would a gorgeous, successful, charming man who, she imagined, could have any woman he wanted see in her—a skinny, forty-two-year-old widow with a flat chest and a bump in her nose!

CHAPTER TWO

THE next fortnight passed in a blur for Maggie.
Despite Juliet's insistence that she felt one hundred per cent well Maggie knew she was still
far from fully recovered. Juliet's ex-husband
was away on a training exercise with the
Australian navy and being a single mother was
hard enough when you were fit and healthy, let
alone when you were recovering from surgery.
Maggie understood that and it was why she was
in Melbourne, to take some of the pressure off
her sister. Juliet's children were at school but
it was their extra-curricular activities that had
Maggie run off her feet, and by the time nine-
year-old Kate and six-year-old Edward were in
bed Maggie was looking forward to putting her
feet up and enjoying a glass of wine. Maggie's
niece and nephew were a lot younger than her
own children and she'd forgotten how much
time got eaten up just doing the basics for a

young family. She'd forgotten how exhausting it could be.

'Here's to tomorrow, the start of my new life.' Juliet raised her wine glass in a toast to the future and waited for Maggie to join her. As Maggie's glass clinked against hers Juliet went on. 'And here's to a fresh start for you too.'

'What do you mean?'

'I've discovered there's nothing like coming face to face with your own mortality to make one stop and assess their life. There're still so many things I want to see and do so I'm putting the past two years behind me and putting my energy into my future.' Juliet sipped her wine. 'But thinking about my future got me wondering about yours too. I've been trying to work out where you're headed as well.'

'I'm not sure I'm headed anywhere.'

'That's my point,' Juliet replied. 'You should be. I think you need to take stock of your life too. I think everyone should. We should all have a five- or ten-year plan.'

'What ten-year plan?'

'The one we're going to work out tonight. Your kids are adults now and they'll be busy with their own lives. You should have a list of a thousand things you've always wanted to do but never had time for. Now's your chance to start on that list—you just have to work out what to do first.'

'I've been thinking about doing some courses, taking up a hobby,' Maggie admitted.

Juliet snickered.

'What?' Maggie asked.

'I was thinking more of long-term things, more about your life for the foreseeable future, not just the next few months.'

'You asked what was on my list.'

'Maybe I should have been more specific. Who do you want to do those things with? You're forty-two—you could potentially live for another forty years. You're not going to spend those years alone, are you?'

Juliet must be feeling better, Maggie decided; she was back to her bossy self! 'You could be in the same position, you know. Merry widow, gay divorcée—either way we're both single,' she retorted.

'Don't think I haven't thought about that,' Juliet said. 'Leaving Sam was one of the hardest things I've ever done but I haven't accepted that I'll never find love again. And I hate to think of *you* spending the rest of your life alone.'

'I thought I could move in with you. Once your kids have flown the nest we could be two old-maid sisters living out their last days in peace and quiet,' Maggie joked.

'Speak for yourself—*I* don't intend to spend my twilight years alone. It's too soon for me but I think *you* need to start dating.'

'I've been on dates.'

'When was your last date?' Juliet asked.

'Just before I came down to Melbourne.'

'How many third dates have you had?'

Maggie was silent—third dates were few and far between. Most of the time a second date was as far as things went before she decided there was no chemistry, attraction or even the pos- sibility of intelligent conversation and called it quits.

'Thought so,' Juliet responded, interpreting her silence. 'And when was the last time you had sex?'

'I don't remember.'

Juliet threw her hands up into the air, almost

spilling her wine in the process. 'That's my point exactly—you should remember. It should have been recent and it should have been fantastic. You need to get out more.'

Maggie twirled her wine glass in her hands. 'Do you want to know why I don't date? For the first twelve months after Steven died no one knew what to do with me. I didn't get invited anywhere. Everyone assumed I needed time to deal with my grief but what they didn't realize was that the lack of invitations meant I had more time than I knew what to do with, more time to think about what I'd lost. When I finally got invited out again I got the feeling that half the women thought I'd be after their husbands. It made me uncomfortable. It was easier not to go to some things.'

'Don't you meet people at work?'

'I don't want to date people from work,' Maggie replied. 'It's too complicated.'

'What about people you meet *through* work?'

'Like who? Patients?' She laughed. 'I work in Theatre, remember? I only see patients for a few minutes before they go under anaesthetic and then they're off to Recovery before they really wake up. Not much opportunity to start chatting, other than telling them to count backwards from twenty!' Maggie shook her head. 'I'm not against the idea of romance or even a simple roll in the hay but in my opinion dating takes too much effort. A hobby would be much easier.'

'Back to that!' Juliet sighed. 'You know you don't necessarily have to date if all you want is a bit of romp.'

But that wasn't really how Maggie operated. She knew she was someone who wanted the whole experience—attraction, romance, a strong connection both emotionally and physically. That was exactly why she was still on her own, why she didn't often go on third dates. She was still waiting for the perfect man to sweep her off her feet, just as Steven had done more than twenty years ago. But was Juliet right? Was she being too fussy? Was she looking at spending the next forty years alone?

Working and being a sole parent for the past ten years had drained her, but when she thought of Juliet's life hers seemed blessed in comparison. Juliet had been through a divorce, a malignant breast lump, chemotherapy, a double mastectomy and then a near-death experience. Just one of those things would be more than most people could cope with, Maggie thought, let alone all of them.

'You deserve to have some fun after the past two years you've had,' she said to Juliet.

'What about you? Don't you want to have fun?'

'I'm happy as I am.' Was that true? What was her definition of happy? Her own children made her happy—most of the time, she thought with a smile. Her extended family. Her work. But was that enough?

'Don't you think you could be happier?' Juliet wanted to know.

Maggie shrugged. She wasn't sure this was a conversation she wanted to have.

But Juliet wasn't finished yet. 'I have a suggestion for you. I know you've come to Melbourne to help me but you don't need to stay home twenty-four hours a day on my account. If I can introduce you to some decent single men, would you go out on a date?'

'Why?'

'Because you might have fun! I'm not ready to get out and about yet but that doesn't mean we both have to sit at home. I'm quite happy to live vicariously through you for the time being. Nobody in Melbourne knows you and your story—it's a good chance to relax and enjoy yourself.'

'Who are these single men you have in mind?' Maggie wasn't about to agree to Juliet's plans without more information.

'You can choose.'

'Me?'

Juliet nodded. 'I know a few single men. Besides, I have an ulterior motive. If I can find you someone perfect you might end up staying in Melbourne, close to me,' she said with a grin.

'Why am I not surprised?' Maggie said. 'There's always a grand plan with you!'

'Tell me your idea of a perfect man and I'll see what I can do,' Juliet prompted.

Maggie decided she really didn't have anything to lose by agreeing to Juliet's plan. If nothing else, it would keep Juliet off her back, and Maggie had learned a long time ago that letting Juliet think she was winning a battle was one way of ensuring a quiet life. So what would her perfect man look like these days?

Tall and solid, but fit rather than fat. A protector. Someone dependable. Dark hair. Blue eyes. Turquoise blue. An image of Ben McMahon flashed before Maggie's eyes. Tall, dark, gorgeous and obviously intelligent—was it any surprise he sprang to mind?

'Who is it?' Juliet badgered. 'You must have someone in mind—you're daydreaming.'

'I don't know if he's perfect—he seems too good to be true.'

'Sounds interesting. Who?'

'Ben McMahon.'

'Mmm. Good choice. He's pretty close to perfect. Smart, sexy and single.'

'Single?' She hadn't actually expected him to be single. 'So *that's* what's wrong with him.' Maggie sighed.

'What?'

'He's gay.'

Juliet laughed. 'Not as far as I know but why don't you test that theory?'

'How?'

'Ask him out.'

'Hang on a minute—I thought *you* were finding me a date.'

'He wasn't on my list,' Juliet argued, 'but I'm sure we can work something out. Why don't you try flirting with him at my appointment tomorrow, then we'll find out if he's interested.'

Maggie got embarrassed at the *thought* of flirting with Ben. She couldn't possibly do it for real without making a complete spectacle of herself, could she?

'Are you sure he's not married?' she clarified. That would be too humiliating and just her luck.

'Trust me, he's single and he's straight.'

'How do you know?'

'He's always in the social pages—his family is Melbourne high society—and he's always with a different woman in every photo. I'm sure that's not just camouflage, and if he had a wife I'm certain she wouldn't be putting up with that!'

'What do you mean, 'high society'?' Maggie's curiosity was piqued.

'His father's family owns a publishing company and his mother runs the McMahon Foundation. Even in Sydney you would have heard of them, surely?'

'He's one of *those* McMahons?'

Juliet nodded and Maggie felt sick at the thought of trying to have a normal conversation with Ben now, let alone flirt with the man. He would have women throwing themselves at him at every opportunity, and she didn't want to put herself in that same category. 'I don't know. He's way out of my league.'

'Don't be ridiculous, you need to stop thinking like that right now. You're good enough for anyone. Besides, I'm only asking you to flirt with the guy—he doesn't need to propose.'

But appreciating a fine example when it crossed her path was one thing; drawing attention to herself was another thing entirely.

As she rinsed out the wine glasses and got ready for bed she reflected on what she'd just agreed to. Juliet wanted to have fun; Maggie wanted to be happy.

She didn't want to be lonely but she very much doubted that Ben McMahon held the key to her happiness. She shrugged her shoulders. She supposed she had nothing to lose by flirting a little. What was the worst that could happen?

Maggie hesitated over applying make-up the next morning as she got ready to take Juliet for her first post-op appointment with Dr McMahon. Ben.

She wasn't as completely out of practice as Juliet might think. It had been years after Steven had died before she'd even contemplated dating but she had been on a few dates in the past five years. It was just that she hadn't enjoyed them particularly. When that was the case she couldn't see the point of continuing to date, of waiting to see if she 'grew to like them'. She knew she wouldn't, so while she *had* dated, it could certainly be said she hadn't had a proper relationship since Steven had died.

She reminded herself that the aim of today wasn't to get Ben to ask her out on a date; she just needed to make a little light conversation, just to show she was trying. She didn't necessarily want to draw attention to herself but she decided a bit of make-up might help her feel more in control of the situation.

Her hand shook as she tried to apply her lip-gloss. She was as nervous as she could ever remember being. All because she was supposed to flirt with a gorgeous man! She ignored the eyeshadow, thinking it would be overkill for a morning appointment, and just put some eye drops into her eyes to dull any traces of red. She brushed her dark hair until it shone and debated over whether to tie it up but in the end she left it down, falling over her shoulders. The brushstrokes were relaxing but she was still terrified she'd embarrass herself despite Juliet's assurances that men would either be flattered by, or ignorant of, her methods.

Maybe if she failed spectacularly Juliet would let her off the hook. She thought she might prefer being lonely to being terrified.

But she needed to at least look as though she was trying. And she was still a woman—she still wanted to see if she could catch a man's eye, even if she wasn't quite sure what she wanted to do next. Everyone's ego needed a boost now and then; she wasn't really any dif-

ferent to the next person. She decided to make
an effort.

She searched through her clothes looking
for a bra that wasn't more than three years old
and that managed to lift her boobs back up to
somewhere close to where they used to be. She
pulled a dress out of the wardrobe, holding it
in front of her—too fancy for a doctor's appointment she decided. Jeans? Too casual. She
swapped the jeans for a skirt that gave a little
bit of shape to her boyish figure and put on a
fitted T-shirt—white—to make it look as if her
boobs were bigger than they really were. That
looked better. Finally she was ready.

Maggie sat in the waiting room, convinced everyone could hear her heart hammering in her
chest. She wiped her clammy hands on her skirt
and looked for something to distract her.

'What do you think of these?'

Maggie glanced at the photograph in the magazine her sister was holding.

'Pamela Anderson! Is that what you chose?'
Maggie knew her younger sister had gotten
the flamboyant gene whereas she'd inherited

the conservative one but, even so, she hadn't expected her to choose to be quite so out there. 'You're not serious! I thought you wanted to look like the old you?'

Juliet grinned at her. 'You're right, classy, not brassy. I picked out boobs that look more like Kate Winslet's.' Juliet turned back a page and showed Maggie another photo.

'Huh!'

'What?' Juliet asked.

'I didn't realise when you said the "old you," you really meant the "young you." Kate's boobs look like yours did in your teens, not what they looked like in your thirties after a couple of kids!' Maggie couldn't resist teasing her sister; some light-hearted banter was just what she needed to distract her from Juliet's 'mission.'

'You think her boobs are too good for me?'

'Not at all, it's just that they're not at all saggy.'

Juliet took the magazine back and had another look at the photo, her forehead creasing a little as she studied it. 'Why is that, do you think? She's had two kids as well.' She paused, tilting her head slightly to one side. 'Could be a flattering angle or a good bra.'

'Or she could have had work done,' Maggie said.

'That does it, I'm definitely getting boobs like hers, then—particularly if they look natural and they're not! Not much point in saggy new boobs.'

Maggie glanced down at her own chest. She'd never been more than a B-cup and she'd never considered being anything else—as long as everything worked, that was all that mattered, as far as she was concerned. But even though she wasn't about to change her own body, which had served her well for forty-two years, she could see Juliet's point. 'I suppose, if you're going to have a breast reconstruction, you might as well get what you want.'

'My thoughts exactly.' Juliet chuckled.

'Come through, Juliet.' Ben appeared in the waiting room and Maggie was surprised by the pull of attraction she felt. He was wearing a white shirt with no tie; his collar was open at his throat, and as Maggie stood she could see a smattering of dark hair below his collarbones. 'You sound in good spirits.'

'Just showing Maggie which boobs I've ordered.' Juliet gestured towards her sister. 'You remember Maggie, don't you?'

'Of course. Are you feeling the pressure of providing a second opinion?' His eyes met hers, holding her attention. There was something in the way he looked at her that made her go weak at the knees. She got the feeling he could read her mind, could see into her soul. Her heartbeat increased its pace.

She couldn't do this! She knew she'd get flustered and make a fool of herself. There was an energy that surrounded him, and she was much too attracted to him to flirt comfortably. In the two weeks since she'd seen him she'd forgotten just how good-looking he was.

But he was waiting for her response. She said the first thing that popped into her head. 'Someone had to make sure Juliet didn't end up looking like Pamela Anderson.' She went for levity in her reply in an attempt to break the spell Ben seemed to have over her. If she could crack a joke maybe she'd be able to breathe again and maybe her heart would be able to return to its normal rhythm.

So far, so good. Her voice sounded normal, no squeaks or breathlessness.

He smiled. There was a definite sparkle in his eyes and that was all it took for her heart to start racing again. 'That was an option?' he asked as he led them through to his office.

She answered quickly while his back was turned, before he had another opportunity to throw her off kilter. 'Not for long!'

'Don't tell fibs, Mags,' Juliet said as she sat in one of the chairs in front of Ben's desk and placed the magazine on the table, tapping a photograph. 'I'd like to look like Kate Winslet, please.'

Ben picked up the magazine. 'Kate Winslet? What do you think, Maggie?' He lifted his gaze to hers, his blue eyes focusing on her and making her stomach somersault. If he kept looking at her like that she'd never be able to answer.

She tore her gaze away, concentrating on the photograph. 'Far more suitable than Pamela,' she replied.

'Pamela might have been fun though,' Juliet said.

'I'm sure you'd find those boobs more annoying than fun after a while, not to mention the backache.' That was better. She should concentrate on Juliet; she could talk to her like a normal person!

'Oh, Mags, you're such a sensible older sister.'

'Be nice or I'll get Ben to give you the saggy version of Kate.'

'You wouldn't dare!'

Maggie stuck out her tongue and Ben laughed. The sound washed over Maggie. She'd made him laugh and it was the nicest sound she'd heard in a long time. Deep and rich, he laughed like a man who enjoyed himself, like a man who laughed often and easily.

'Sorry, girls, I'd prefer not to do saggy and I wouldn't give Juliet "Pammy" breasts either. Neither option would be good for my reputation.'

Ben's comment took Maggie by surprise. She thought all men would choose Pamela Anderson if they got the chance. And he looked as if he'd prefer American-type women. Blonde, blue-eyed, white teeth and big boobs—cheer-leaders.

What was she doing? Why was she even con-sidering what type of women he'd like? His taste in women was of no concern to her, although she'd bet his taste didn't lean towards skinny, small-breasted, brunette Aussie women!

Stop it—who cares? she thought, knowing, even as she asked herself the question, that she did.

This flirting thing was going to end in disaster unless she got her hormones under control.

Ben was talking to Juliet now, the consulta-tion under way, leaving Maggie time to settle her nerves. 'A good C-cup will suit you per-fectly Juliet, as we've discussed. That's assum-ing the tissue expander stretches enough over the next few weeks to allow me to put C-cup implants in. Have you had any soreness or no-ticed any redness over the past few days?'

'No, everything's settled down well.'

'Excellent. If you're ready to get started I'll get you to go behind the screen, slip your shirt off and lie down on the bed. There's a sheet there to put over you.'

Juliet disappeared behind the privacy screen, and Ben went to the sink to wash his hands before pulling on a pair of disposable gloves.

Maggie could hear him explaining the process to Juliet as he worked. She listened to him while she studied his office.

'Everything looks good. I'm planning to inject about ninety millilitres of saline into the tissue expander today if I can. Remember, the whole process will take six to eight weeks as each injection stretches the expander a little more until we can replace it with the implants. How many weeks exactly will depend on how easily your skin stretches.'

Maggie scanned the artwork on the walls. There had been a definite African theme to the pictures in the waiting room and that continued in Ben's office where several stunning photographs were displayed on the walls. She told herself she was interested in the photos for art's sake but she knew the truth. The truth was she was looking for clues about Ben, about his life outside of work. She was snooping. But the artwork told her nothing except that he seemed to have an interest in Africa.

'I'll do the left side first. It won't hurt—there are no nerve endings so you won't feel the saline going in. It goes straight into the expander through the skin valve. You might feel a little stretching but that should be about it.'

Maggie's gaze travelled to the desk. There were a few pieces of African art—sculptures and the like on his desk and bookshelf—but no photos, particularly no photos that could be of a wife, or ex-wife, and children.

So Juliet was right...Ben was single?

'OK, almost done. You might find it gets a little uncomfortable over the next twenty-four hours or so as the muscles stretch. Take some mild analgesics if you need to.'

Maggie heard Ben snap his gloves off and then he reappeared from behind the privacy screen.

'Are you able to help Juliet for the next twenty-four hours, Maggie? I'd like her to avoid driving, heavy lifting and raising her arms above chest height for the next day, just to help prevent any additional soreness.'

'Yes, I'm still staying at her house.'

'Great,' he said as Juliet joined them in front of the screen. 'I'll see you both next Friday, then?'

'Definitely,' Juliet said, jumping in before Maggie had a chance to reply.

Ben opened the door for them but didn't follow them out.

'There you go—that wasn't so hard, was it?' Juliet asked as they returned to the reception desk to confirm her remaining appointments. 'And he sounds like he's looking forward to seeing you next week too.'

'I'm sure he's just making polite conversation.'

'Time will tell,' Juliet said with a grin.

Maggie sensed she had more to add but fortunately they were now back in the waiting area and Juliet seemed to decide not to share her opinion with the rest of Ben's patients, or his staff. But Juliet's comment got Maggie thinking as she waited for the receptionist to confirm the next appointment—did she want Ben's remark to be genuine? She was sure it had been said with sincerity—she didn't doubt

that—but did she want him to be looking forward to seeing her again specifically? That
thought made her equally nervous and excited
and she found herself replaying his words
many times over the course of the evening
before finally deciding it was what it was—a
polite comment with no hidden agenda! As
much as she hated to admit it, disappointment
accompanied that realisation.

CHAPTER THREE

IT WAS a busy Saturday morning in Hawthorn and Maggie was feeling a little frazzled after trying to find a car park around Glenferrie Oval, where vacant spots were as rare as the proverbial hen's teeth.

'OK, champ, let's get in the line to hand in your registration,' she said to Edward as they joined the queue stretching around the perimeter of the oval.

It was her nephew's first football-coaching clinic and Maggie had offered to bring him as Juliet was still feeling tender and sore following the tissue expander procedure the day before.

There seemed to be hundreds of six-year-olds running amok all over the oval and dozens of footballs were whizzing through the air in all directions. The grass was a mass of brown and gold as most children were wearing miniature versions of the local football team's tops.

'Can you do it, Auntie Maggie? My friends are over there kicking the footy.' Edward pointed across the oval and looked up at her with his best pleading expression.

What should she do? If it were her own child she'd say yes in a flash but Maggie didn't know Edward's friends and didn't really know what today's procedure was.

'Please?' he begged.

'Which friends?'

'Jake and Rory.' He pointed at a group of children, all in brown-and-yellow football jerseys. Maggie couldn't tell one from the other, but she remembered meeting one of Juliet's friends, Anna, who had a son called Jake. She could only assume that was who Edward was talking about.

The oval was fenced and Edward didn't seem bothered. In fact, he seemed rather keen to run off. Maggie shrugged. 'I guess that's all right but just listen when they call you in for the start of the session, OK? I'll sit in the grandstand and watch.'

Edward nodded his head and disappeared, leaving Maggie to stand in line to register

before she could make her way to the old grandstand.

'Morning, Maggie.'

She had just sat down in the front row of the
grandstand where she could bask in the autumn
sun when she heard the greeting. She hadn't
expected anyone to recognise her here. She certainly hadn't expected to know anyone herself,
but that voice was instantly recognisable.

'Ben! What are you doing here?' A thousand
questions raced through Maggie's mind in the
space of a few short seconds. The questions
seemed to be keeping time with her heartbeat.
And as quickly as her heart had begun racing
it stopped and sank in her chest as she realised why he was here. 'Do you have children
here?'

He shook his head. 'A nephew. You?'

Her heart leapt back up to its rightful spot.
'Same. I brought Juliet's son.'

'Are you staying to watch the session?' he
asked and when Maggie nodded he continued.
'Can I get you a coffee? I was just on my way
for one.'

A warm glow spread through her. She wouldn't

say no to Ben's company. Juliet's plan sprang to mind and while she certainly couldn't call this a date it did involve striking up a conversation. Who knew, maybe she *could* flirt with him. And let's face it, she told herself, if she couldn't flirt with someone who literally made her toes curl with desire there wasn't much hope for her, was there?

'That would be lovely, thank you.'

'Cappuccino, latte, flat white?'

'You don't suppose they'd make a hot chocolate?' she asked.

He smiled at her—yep, her toes were curling—and said, 'I'll see what I can do,' before he headed off towards the coffee van.

'One hot chocolate,' he said on his return, handing her a takeaway cup and a paper bag, 'and a blueberry muffin. I'm eating so I took a chance on your preference.'

Maggie peeked into the bag, 'Looks great, thanks.'

'Here, let me hold the muffin while you take the lid off your drink.' Ben's fingers brushed against her hand as he took the bag from her, and she almost dropped the cup when a trail of heat raced up her arm. Her hand shook as she removed the lid to allow her drink to cool down but Ben seemed oblivious to her sudden bout of nerves. 'Which one is your nephew?' he asked.

Maggie shielded her eyes with one hand as she sought out Edward. She'd left her sunglasses in the car. The day had started off grey and bleak, and she'd forgotten how rapidly Melbourne weather changed.

'Is the sun bothering you? Did you want to move further back in the grandstand?' Ben asked.

'No. I'm enjoying the sun. I'm finding Melbourne mornings a bit chilly, to be honest. I need some sunshine to warm me up.'

'Are you not from here?'

'I'm from Sydney. I've just come down to help Juliet with the kids while she was having surgery.'

'Did you grow up here or there?'

If she'd had a thousand questions when she'd first seen Ben this morning it seemed as though he had more! 'Sydney, born and bred,' she replied. 'Juliet moved here with her ex-husband.

He's in the navy and she stayed when they split up. Kate, her daughter, was settled in school and Juliet figured that was easier than moving.'

'How long are you here for?'

'I've taken some long service leave and I might go back and forward a bit until she's had the implants. It sort of depends on how she goes with the procedures.' She held his gaze. 'I guess it's up to you a bit, isn't it?'

'Maybe I should take my time,' he said. 'Give you a chance to enjoy our hospitality.' He smiled and his blue eyes sparkled, reminding her of the ocean on a sunny day.

She couldn't believe it—was he flirting back? Maybe his farewell after Juliet's appointment hadn't been simply polite rhetoric? Before she had time to work that out Ben had moved on in the conversation.

'Speaking of Juliet, how is she going?'

She decided she didn't have the skills to work out whether or not Ben was flirting so she stuck to the script. 'She's a bit sore today. She says she feels as though she's done too many push-ups, so I guess it's muscular soreness she's de-scribing.'

'She hasn't had any other side effects?'

'Physically or emotionally?'

'Either.'

'Not really. I expected her to be a bit tired from the surgery and the near-death experience but she seems to have bounced back with more energy than ever. She's even more determined to make the most of every moment now. She's been a bit like that since she finished chemo after the mastectomy but it's more noticeable now. She would have come with me today except she's taken her daughter to a ballet class.' Ben opened his mouth to speak out but Maggie guessed what he was about to ask and added, 'Don't worry, she didn't have to drive. It's walking distance.'

'So she doesn't seem worried about what happened in Theatre?'

'No, she seems fine, quite calm about the whole thing considering.'

'Considering what?'

'The fact she says she heard my husband's voice.'

Husband? Ben's eyes flicked to Maggie's left hand. She was wearing a wedding ring. He'd noticed her; how had he not noticed her wedding ring?

'Is it possible she could have heard him?' His mind was buzzing but somehow he managed to formulate a reply.

She shrugged. 'It's not impossible. He died ten years ago.'

So she was widowed. Had she remarried? Was that why she was wearing a ring? Questions whirled around in his head. While newly single women were definitely fair game in his opinion, married women definitely were not. But when had he put Maggie in his sights? He knew the answer to that. Yesterday—when he'd spent too much time thinking about her when he should have been writing reports. He was supposed to have been entering details of Juliet's procedure into her file but his mind had kept drifting, not aimlessly but rather definitely, to Maggie.

She was a stunning woman. As a plastic surgeon he was trained to notice bone structure and Maggie had a perfect oval face and fabulous cheekbones. Even the bump in the bridge of her nose, that she apparently hated, gave her face character. He'd been honest when he said he wouldn't change it.

Her eyes were a startling blue, and as he looked into them now he could picture her in Theatre. Gowned, masked, capped—covered up except for her eyes. He wondered how the other staff kept focused.

He shook his head to clear his mind and ran back over the events in his theatre. He couldn't remember everything—it had all happened very quickly—but some things were clear. 'Was his name Steven?'

'Yes.' Maggie's brow creased with concentration as she looked at him, or was it confusion? 'How did you know that?'

'When we'd revived her I asked her if she could hear me and she called me Steven. At least, I thought she was talking to me.'

Maggie shook her head. 'She thinks she was talking to my husband.'

'You're a nurse, a theatre nurse, you said?' He waited for her confirmation. 'Do you think there's something to these "near-death experiences," for want of a better term?'

'I've heard too many reports to be able to discount them completely.'

'Really? You've had other patients report similar things? Firsthand experiences?'

Maggie nodded. 'Three or four times, I reckon. And there have been plenty of similarities between them. The light, the feeling of peace and tranquillity, hearing loved ones.'

'So what's your opinion, then?'

'I've often wondered about it, from both sides—the emotional and the physiological. I can see the scientists' point of view—they say it's all chemical reaction and nerve synapses— but when Juliet said she'd heard Steven's voice, that all made sense too. But maybe she just confused someone else's voice with his, maybe it was you she could hear. Do you remember what you said? If you can remember it could explain whether she heard you or not.'

He shook his head. 'I don't remember anything specific, it was all rather frantic. I was more interested in trying to save her life than in paying attention to what I was saying. I would have been talking to her, trying to get her to hold on, but more than that I couldn't say. I've never had one of my patients flatline before. I was more concerned about saving her.'

'Well, I'm very glad you did. I don't think I could bear to lose Juliet, not after all she's been through.' Maggie smiled at him as she spoke but her smile was tinged with sadness, and Ben knew she was thinking of more than just Juliet's close call. Maggie had lost someone she loved before, and he wondered if she had found love again. 'And, as for near-death experiences, I'd like to think they're real.'

'The white light and the voices… You think people are waiting to guide us to heaven?'

She shrugged her shoulders and her dark hair shone as the sunlight bounced off it showing up shades of red and gold amongst the predominantly dark waves. 'I don't know about heaven but I believe there's another life waiting for us after this one. I think it's likely to be very different but I need to believe there is something. Even if it's just a place where souls can meet again. But that's just my opinion. I'm still not sure if Juliet's recollection gives any more weight to my theory.'

'It's a nice idea though.'

'Yes, it is.' Maggie's eyes met his and for a moment neither of them spoke. He understood her need to believe in an afterlife, in whatever form it came. As a doctor he'd seen that belief get people through some horrendous situations. This sharing of opinions forged a connection between them that didn't need words. He kept eye contact, amazed again at just how blue her eyes were, their unusual colour accentuated by her dark eyelashes. Other than the bump in her nose her features were remarkably symmetrical and gave her a slight ethereal quality.

'Thank you for listening.' Maggie put a hand on his arm. It was an unconscious gesture on her part—he'd swear she was completely un-aware of the movement—but the touch of her palm on his bare forearm sent a surge of desire through him that took him by surprise.

She was an attractive woman—physically not more so than a dozen others he knew—but this spark that zipped through him was un-usual. There had to be some scientific reason for it; in his mind there was a scientific reason for everything. Even near-death experiences, in his opinion, were simply a by-product of a person's wiring. Not that he'd pushed that idea on Maggie; he'd been too interested in her thoughts. But chemistry between two people, two strangers, that was stuff of fiction. The spark must simply be due to ions in their bodies or the humidity in the air. Something simple. Something scientific.

'Look what I got, Uncle Ben.'

An unexpected voice startled him. His nephew was standing in front of him, proudly displaying a bright yellow football and a backpack.

'Rory! Has the clinic finished?' He hadn't noticed the session coming to an end.

'Rory is your nephew?' Maggie said. 'My nephew Edward's friend? Why didn't you say something?'

He turned to Maggie—he must have missed some information along the way. 'I didn't know there was a connection,' he admitted. 'I know that my sister, Gabby, recommended me to Juliet but I didn't think to ask how they knew each other. It must be through the boys' school.' He paused, wondering if this information gave him licence to take another step, before deciding there was only one way to find out. 'We're going to have a milkshake now, why don't you join us?'

'Thank you, we'd love to but we can't. I made a deal with Juliet that if she wanted to walk Kate to ballet I'd pick her up afterwards. We'll have to get going.'

That was OK—she hadn't knocked him back. 'Maybe next week, then.'

'Will you be bringing Rory again?'

'More than likely. My sister and her husband travel quite often for their business, and I help my parents out with Rory on weekends when I can.'

'That's very good of you.'

'Not at all, I think I get more out of it than Rory. He's great company.'

'So, next Saturday, then?' she said with a smile which he found ridiculously satisfying.

He nodded, pleased she seemed keen to join him, and as he watched her walking away, a slim figure in faded jeans, he tried again to work out what it was about her that appealed to him. He thought back over their conversation. She'd been very open and honest; he guessed there'd be no game playing with her.

Perhaps that was her point of difference—she was genuine. Could it be that simple?

As he caught the last glimpse of her as she and Edward left the oval he realised he was already looking forward to next week. She intrigued him, he decided, and he couldn't recall the last time he'd been able to say that about someone.

Maggie listened to Edward recount the morning's activities to Juliet as she heated soup for lunch and prepared sandwiches. He didn't mention Ben, but then why would he? Football had been the big attraction for him.

'Was it as much fun as Edward thinks?' Juliet asked her when she came into the kitchen. 'It didn't drag on for too long?'

'Not at all,' Maggie answered. The time had passed in the blink of an eye.

'Did you have to help out?'

Maggie shook her head. 'No, there were plenty of official helpers. It was pretty well organised.'

'What did you do for an hour, then?'

'Ben McMahon was there,' Maggie said,

hoping she sounded calm despite her sizzling nerves. 'I chatted to him.'

Juliet squealed. 'What did you talk about?'

My dead husband, Maggie thought, knowing that Juliet would have a fit if she admitted this had been a topic of conversation; that was surely a no-go zone in the 'art of flirting.' She decided to keep that to herself and went with, 'This and that—the kids. Ben said that Rory's parents are away—something to do with their work?' She changed the subject.

'I'd forgotten they're interstate. They run a rather successful art gallery in St Kilda and they focus on indigenous art, Aboriginal and other cultures. They travel a lot.' Juliet paused and Maggie could almost see the wheels turning in her head. 'You should get Ben to show you their gallery.'

'I think he'd have better things to do.'

'You'll never know until you ask.'

Maggie could have told Juliet then all about their conversation but she knew it was too complicated to explain how she'd immediately felt comfortable in Ben's company. How it hadn't felt strange to talk to Ben about Steven or about such a controversial subject as life after death and people's perceptions of heaven.

Talking to Ben she'd felt as though her opinion mattered, as though it was worth something. She was an intensely private sort of person, much more so than Juliet, so to have such a revealing conversation with a virtual stranger must say something about Ben. Or maybe it said more about her feelings towards Ben, and she wasn't ready to share those yet. Not even with Juliet.

Nor was she about to mention the plans for next weekend. She wanted to hug that to herself for a little longer. It felt too precious, and she knew that sharing the news would diminish that. So she just shrugged and concentrated on making lunch and steered the conversation back to Juliet's morning and then onto their plans and schedule for the following week. It had been a while since her own children had depended on her for everything, and Maggie wanted to make sure she had a handle on what needed to happen in order for Juliet's household to run smoothly. The kids had had enough upheaval, and Maggie wanted to make things easy for everyone. Focusing on what everyone else needed also meant she didn't have time to examine her own feelings too closely.

But over the next week Maggie's thoughts kept returning to Ben with rather alarming frequency. Folding laundry, washing dishes, chatting to Juliet, driving the children around town—no activity was immune and it was a strange sensation to have her mind wandering off on its own tangent.

Her reaction to Ben scared her a little; she barely knew the man. How was it he could have such a strong impact on her?

'I missed you at Juliet's appointment yesterday.'

Maggie was standing at the edge of the football oval, having just sent Edward to join his training group, and she turned at the sound of Ben's voice, a smile already on her face.

Her breath caught in her throat as she met his eyes. He hadn't shaved this morning and his square jaw was darkened by stubble and the blue of his eyes was heightened by the shadow of his beard. He was seriously gorgeous. He was holding two takeaway coffee cups, and her eyes were drawn to his hands as he offered her a cup. The cups looked small in his grasp but although his hands were large they weren't chunky. His fingers were slender, his nails clean and nicely shaped. 'One hot chocolate for you.'

'Thank you,' she replied, touched he'd remembered her order. She'd spent countless hours over the previous week rehearsing what she'd say to Ben when she saw him next, running through all the topics one might consider suitable for conversation—work, movies, books, sport. The only trouble was she wasn't working, she hadn't had time to go to the movies or read, and she really knew nothing about football— and to admit that to a Melbournian was social suicide. Maybe Ben could teach her about football? In the meantime she'd have to stick with talking about the children. 'I couldn't make Juliet's appointment yesterday,' she explained in reply to his initial comment. 'I went to school assembly instead. Kate's class was doing a presentation.'

Ben nodded. 'Juliet told me.'

Ben had asked Juliet where she was? A thrill of excitement snaked its way through Maggie's stomach at the thought.

'She also told me that you enjoyed last week's football clinic so much you'd volunteered to come again today,' Ben continued.

Maggie could feel the heat suffusing her cheeks and cursed her fair skin as the blush spread across her face. She made a show of looking out across the oval, pretending to watch the children chasing after footballs, anything to avoid looking directly at Ben and letting him see how embarrassed she was. 'What else did she tell you?'

'That you don't need to rush off after today's session. Which means you and Edward are free to join us for a milkshake.'

She smiled, pleased the invitation was still there. 'We hadn't forgotten.'

'Is Juliet here as well?' he asked as, in silent agreement, they made their way up the stairs of the grandstand to sit in the same seats as last week.

Maggie shook her head. 'No, she said it was too cold this morning. She's at home.' Maggie silently wondered whether Juliet had deliberately used the weather as an excuse but then realised she didn't care. She was actually pleased to have Ben's company to herself. She'd promised herself she'd try to have a more cheerful conversation this week though—no talk of dead husbands or gruesome hospital tales—and she intended to remain full of good news and optimism. She was about to ask him how his week had been when her mobile phone rang, interrupting her train of thought.

As Maggie excused herself to answer her phone Ben grabbed the chance to study her. He hadn't been surprised to hear that Maggie had enjoyed his company last Saturday—without being conceited he knew he could be good company when he chose—but he had been surprised to find how pleased he was to hear that information. Surprised to realise how much he was looking forward to seeing her again too.

'Everything OK?' he asked when Maggie returned. He hoped Juliet wasn't calling her home for something.

'Fine. That was Sophie, my daughter,' Maggie explained as she sat beside him.

Her daughter? Had he known she had a daughter? He couldn't remember any being mentioned. 'Who's looking after her while you're here?'

Maggie smiled. 'They're OK on their own.'

'What?' She had more than one child? 'They're on their own?'

She was smiling at him; his confusion seemed to be amusing her. 'Sophie is almost twenty-one. James is nineteen.'

How old?

'Are they your stepchildren?' he asked.

'Stepchildren?'

The conversation seemed to be spoken in riddles. 'You can't possibly have children that old.' He looked at her wedding ring. 'You're wearing a ring—I assumed you'd remarried.'

'I haven't remarried.'

She was twisting her wedding ring around on her finger. Ben wanted to ask her more but she was looking out across the oval, not meeting his eyes, and he knew now wasn't the time. He'd ask her about her children instead—in his experience all mothers loved to talk about their kids.

'What do your children do? Are they working, studying, travelling?'

'James is doing vet science and Sophie's— Oh, no!'

Ben followed Maggie's gaze. She was watching Edward's group as they were doing marking practice. Edward was sliding along the ground to scoop up a ball in his arms. It was a difficult catch, one Ben thought he'd managed well—until he couldn't stop his slide. Edward overshot the edge of the oval and crashed into the boundary fence right in front of the grandstand. His head collided with the metal post in the wire-mesh fence. Ben saw his forehead split open like a ripe tomato and blood pour from the wound.

Maggie was rooted to the spot. Ben pushed past her and raced down the grandstand steps, clearing the low boundary fence with a quick jump. Edward was sitting up, holding his hands in front of him and staring silently at the blood as it ran from his forehead and into his hands. Ben knelt beside him, pushing the hair from

Ed's forehead to inspect the damage. There was a nasty gash about three inches long running down the centre of his forehead.

He pulled a clean handkerchief from his pocket and pressed it against the wound. He looked around, looking for an extra pair of hands, looking for assistance, looking for Maggie. She was standing behind his left shoulder.

'Maggie.'

She didn't answer.

'Maggie,' he repeated. 'Can you find me a first-aid kit?' She was staring back at him but her gaze was blank. He needed her to focus but he couldn't get her attention.

Several other parents had gathered around and one of them spoke up. 'I'll find someone for you.'

Ben nodded in acknowledgement before turning his attention back to Ed. He'd worry about Maggie later.

'Edward, can you look at me?' he asked.

Edward lifted his head and looked up. Ben checked his eyes, looking to see if his pupils were equally dilated.

'Do you know where you are, Ed?'

'At footy.'

'Can I get through? I've got the first-aid kit.' One of the clinic organisers pushed through the throng of kids who were standing around, mesmerised by the gory scene in front of them.

'Pass it to me, I'm a doctor.' Ben took the kit; he wasn't about to relinquish control to someone who possibly had only basic first-aid training. 'Can someone find me a blanket too?' He issued instructions before addressing the children who were still gathered around. 'It's OK, kids, heads bleed a lot. It looks worse than it is.' Now that Ben had stemmed the flow of blood all the kids, other than his nephew, Rory, drifted back to football training, which was obviously more interesting.

Ben kept pressure on Edward's head with one hand as he flicked open the first-aid box with the other.

'Has he got a parent with him?' asked the first-aid officer.

Ben pointed at Maggie with his free hand. 'That's his aunt. Can you ask her to give me a hand? She's a nurse.'

Maggie was standing less than two feet from Ben but if the first-aid officer thought it was odd that Ben didn't ask Maggie himself she didn't comment. Ben needed someone to get Maggie to focus.

'Are you his aunt?' Ben heard the woman ask Maggie. She didn't get an immediate response. She touched Maggie's arm. 'Excuse me, are you with this child?'

Maggie heard her this time but Ben thought she looked surprised to find someone standing in front of her addressing her. Maggie nodded.

'He's asked if you could give him a hand.' The woman indicated Ben. 'You are a nurse?' The uncertainty was clear in her tone.

Ben saw Maggie look down at him.

'Maggie, do you think you could find some sterile pads for me?' He could have asked the first-aid officer to help but he thought Edward might prefer familiar faces. He wondered what the matter was with Maggie. He was worried she'd gone into shock, although the accident seemed too minor to have caused such a reaction.

Maggie knelt beside him and rummaged through the first-aid kit. She found pads and ripped the packets open, holding them out for Ben to take. Her hands were shaking but she was at least able to follow instructions, although she still hadn't spoken.

Ben worked quickly, completely focused on the task at hand, but still managing to talk in a calm, quiet voice to Edward, explaining what he was doing.

Someone passed Maggie a blanket, and she wrapped it around Ed's shoulders.

Rory was still standing behind Ben, watching the proceedings. 'Is he going to be OK?' he asked. A huge lump had appeared on Edward's head, and the gash was like a red mouth in the middle of the egg.

'He'll be fine,' Ben answered, 'but he'll need a few stitches.'

'Shall we call an ambulance?' the official asked.

'I can stitch it, I'm a plastic surgeon. I know Edward's mother.' He turned to Maggie. 'Will Juliet be happy for me to do it?'

Maggie couldn't imagine Juliet would have any objections. She nodded.

'OK, then, let's get this held together as best we can for the moment and then we'll take him to my rooms. Can you open some Steri-Strips for me?'

Having a task to do helped Maggie to focus, and she passed Ben the closures for him to tape across Edward's wound, holding the edges together. A dressing followed and Maggie then wrapped a bandage around Edward's head while Ben held the dressing in place. They worked in sync, Maggie simply following Ben's instructions and somehow managing not to get in his way, until Edward was sufficiently patched up and able to be moved.

'All set,' Ben said as he stood, gathering Edward into his arms. 'Let's get to my surgery and I'll stitch you up properly.'

Maggie quickly packed unused items back into the first-aid kit and balled the rubbish up inside a clean surgical glove and handed it to the official. She did these tasks without thinking, her movements automatic. Now that Ben had got things under control Maggie found her skills returning. As she stood she noticed Rory, still standing beside Ben.

'What about Rory?'

Ben frowned. 'He'll have to come with us.'

'I can take him home with me if you like.'

Maggie looked up and recognised Jake's mum, Anna.

Anna continued to organise the logistics. 'I'll drop the boys off with my husband and then I'll pick Juliet up and bring her to your rooms.'

'If you could take Rory that would help.' Ben turned to his nephew. 'Is that OK, mate? You can go home with Jake and I'll pick you up later?' Ben waited for confirmation from Rory before turning back to Anna. 'We'll ring Juliet and tell her what's happened. I won't take long to patch him up so we'll bring Edward home. I'd be finished before you'd get back with Juliet.'

Maggie followed Ben from the oval, pulling her mobile phone from her bag. She pressed the speed dial to call Juliet, hoping her nerves had settled enough to make it sound as though she had things under control. She knew she'd panicked earlier—thank God Ben had been there.

She knew she'd frozen; despite her years of nursing experience her mind had been a complete blank. As a nurse she should be able to cope with an emergency but she also knew she wasn't good with trauma, especially not if it involved a head injury and a family member. She was a theatre nurse in a private hospital that specialised in elective orthopaedic surgery; emergency medicine was not her speciality, and Ben's presence had been a huge comfort. She was deeply indebted to him.

At the surgery Maggie was amazed at how well Edward coped with the situation. Once again, Maggie knew that was thanks to Ben's composed demeanour. Edward had remained quiet and still while Ben stitched his forehead with tiny, perfect subcutaneous stitches before closing the wound with glue to minimise the scarring. Even when Ben injected the local anaesthetic Edward had barely complained.

Ben had chatted away to Edward while he worked, asking him about the footy clinic and his week at school, and Maggie had been greatly relieved when his answers were accurate and valid. Ed remembered crashing into the fence and also remembered catching the ball just prior to that, which was a good sign. He had a headache but his speech wasn't slurred. His memory seemed fine and his movements appeared normal. As Ben drove them home Maggie tried to make herself relax.

Juliet was waiting in the driveway when Ben and Maggie arrived. She opened the door to cuddle Edward but as she began to lift him out of the car Ben stopped her.

'Hold on, Juliet. I'll carry him. He's too heavy for you after your procedure yesterday.'

Ben lifted him easily, and Maggie marvelled again at how small Edward looked against Ben's bulk. She trailed behind them all as Ben carried Ed to his room, explaining what had happened, and what he'd done, to Juliet on the way.

'He's had some analgesia—he'll probably need a sleep but wake him in an hour or so just to check. He didn't lose consciousness and was lucid so I expect he'll just have a sore head. And a good story.'

'Thanks, Ben. We were so lucky you were there.' Juliet turned to Maggie. 'Can you get

Ben something to eat or drink while I see to Ed?'

'Thanks, but I can't stay. I need to pick up Rory.'

Disappointment flooded through Maggie. She walked him out to his car, trying to keep up a normal conversation while she tried to figure out why she was so affected by him.

'Are you positive you don't have kids of your own? You're so good with them.'

Ben held up his three middle fingers, pressing his little finger down with his thumb. 'I haven't got any hidden away somewhere, Scouts' honour.'

'I don't know what I would have done if you hadn't been there—my mind went completely blank.' She knew why she'd panicked but she couldn't explain that to Ben just yet. 'You were brilliant. How can I thank you?'

'You can have dinner with me.'

'Dinner?'

Ben nodded.

'Why?' Her surprise made her sound far less enthusiastic than she felt!

'It might be a pleasant way to end the day. If

you think Juliet can manage without you, then I think you've earned a night out.'

'Is this dinner, as in a date?' Maggie wasn't sure whether to trust her ears and hated to think she might read something into Ben's invitation that wasn't there.

He nodded.

Still she hesitated; was she brave enough?

'Do you like Italian food?'

'It's my favourite.' She wondered briefly if Juliet had told him that, before dismissing the thought as silly. She wasn't important enough for them to have discussed her likes and dislikes.

'Perfect. There's a fabulous Italian restaurant in Carlton I'll take you to. It's nothing fancy but the food is superb. I'll pick you up at eight.'

'You want to go tonight?'

'Yes, is that a problem?'

'I'd love to have dinner with you but I can't, not tonight. Can I take a rain check?'

Ben looked at her; he was obviously waiting for more of an explanation but how could she explain that she was too frightened to leave Edward? He seemed fine, he wasn't her son and Juliet was home, but Maggie knew she'd be poor company tonight. She needed to stay close to Edward for her own peace of mind.

To his credit, Ben didn't question her further. 'Sure, you must be exhausted. We can do it another time,' was all he said, making a perfect excuse for her.

As he drove away she wondered if he let her off the hook so easily because he had plenty of other options. There were sure to be plenty more fish in his sea. Maggie experienced a momentary pang of regret but it wasn't enough to get her to leave Edward's side.

Curiosity had gotten the better of him. He'd seen Maggie in stressful situations twice now, once after Juliet needed reviving on the operating table and once today. Juliet's was surely the more confronting of the two dramas, yet Maggie had been remarkably calm then, in comparison to today. She was a nurse—she was used to dealing with stressful situations—so he couldn't understand why she'd gone to pieces today over a cut forehead. His curiosity had gotten the better of him and he wanted to know why someone whom he thought was calm, confident and rational had struggled to cope with Edward's injury. Having dinner together might have given him a chance to work her out, to satisfy his curiosity, but now it would have to wait.

CHAPTER FOUR

'MUMMY, Mummy, my head hurts.'

Maggie opened her eyes, waking at the sound of Ed's voice. It was still dark outside, just the faint signs that dawn was coming.

'I'm here, darling, what's wrong? It's Auntie Maggie.' Maggie threw back the quilt and sat up, her senses on full alert. She'd been up and down all through the night checking on Ed and had eventually pulled the trundle bed out, grabbed her quilt and fallen asleep next to Edward's bed. She'd been too worried to sleep soundly though, waking at every little noise.

'I can't move my head.'

She flew out of the trundle bed, anxious to check him. She bent over her nephew, who was sitting up in bed. He looked dreadful—his eyelids were bruised purple and his forehead was swollen and misshapen with a sticky dressing plastered across the middle of it. The dressing had started off white but was stained orange with Betadine and his fringe was matted with blood that Juliet hadn't been able to wash out. He resembled a character from a horror film.

She moved around the bed and saw Edward follow her path with his eyes—just his eyes, his neck was stiff and immobile.

'Does it hurt to move your neck?'

'No. My head is sore but my neck is just stuck.'

Maggie frowned. Could he have fractured or displaced a vertebra yesterday when he'd collided with the fence? What if they'd missed it?

'See if you can slowly turn your head to look out the window?'

Edward turned to face the window but he turned his whole body, twisting from the waist. He moved the way people suffering from a wry neck moved, and Maggie wondered whether he had simply slept awkwardly. He could move his thoracic spine well enough; perhaps he just had some muscle spasm or inflammation in his neck muscles.

Juliet entered the room then; their voices must have woken her. 'What's going on?'

'Ed's neck is stiff, I'm just checking it out,' Maggie explained as she sent her sister a warning glance, telling her not to panic or say anything that might alarm Edward. Maggie was worried enough for both of them. 'Jules, would you get me a torch. Ed, can you open and close your hands for me?'

Maggie watched with relief as Edward did this without difficulty.

'Where does your head hurt?'

Edward reached one hand up towards the bump on his forehead but didn't touch it. 'Where I hit it.'

Juliet had turned on the light before leaving the room and it seemed as though bright light wasn't bothering him but Maggie needed to know for sure. 'You can see OK?' she asked Ed as Juliet came back into the bedroom and handed her a small torch.

'Yeah.'

'I'm just going to check your eyes to make certain. Can you close them both for me and then I'll open one at a time and quickly shine the torch in. I need to see what your eyes do in bright light, OK?'

Maggie was relieved to see both pupils were still reacting equally but that didn't rule out a neck injury, just confirmed that Ed probably hadn't suffered any trauma to his brain.

'That all seems fine,' she said to Juliet. 'I hope it's just muscle spasm—it could be the way he slept. I could palpate his neck but I'm not sure I know what to look for and pressure in the wrong spot might make matters worse.' She was thinking out loud. 'I might just ring Ben and see what he thinks.' She was proud of herself that she hadn't fallen apart this morning, unlike yesterday, but she still wanted Ben's advice. She found the card he'd given her and punched his number into the phone.

'Ben McMahon.' He answered on the third ring but his voice sounded groggy, and she realised she'd woken him. She'd been so focused on Edward she hadn't stopped to think of the time.

'Ben, it's Maggie. Sorry to wake you but I'm worried about Edward.'

'What's the matter?'

She could hear in his voice now that he was awake and giving her his full attention. 'He can't move his neck. I think it might be muscular but I want to get him checked out just in case. Could you tell me where I should take him?'

'What are his other symptoms?'

'He's got a bit of a headache, frontal, over the wound site but his pupils are reacting normally and he's got normal movement and sensation in his extremities. He can turn his thoracic and lumbar spine—he just can't turn his neck.'

'It would be pretty unusual to fracture a vertebra when you hit something front on unless there was a whiplash effect. A fall onto the top of his head or a blow to his neck would be more likely to cause a fracture.' Ben immediately picked up on Maggie's concern but his reckoning made sense and eased Maggie's worries slightly. 'Can you get him to the Hawthorn Sports Medicine Clinic? That will be the closest place for X-rays. You should be all right to drive him, just support his head. I'll meet you there. Can you do that or do you want to call an ambulance?'

'We'll manage, thanks, Ben. We'll see you soon.' Just the fact that he was happy to make decisions, relieving her of some of that burden, helped to set her at ease.

She disconnected the call and went back to the bedroom. 'Ben will meet us at the Hawthorn Sports Medicine Clinic. Do you know where that is?' Juliet nodded. 'What about Kate—do you need to wake her up to come with us?'

'She went to a friend's for a sleepover. She won't be home till lunchtime.' Maggie had forgotten that Kate had gone out; that made things a little easier. 'What do I need to do?' Juliet asked. Maggie balked for a second but of course Juliet would expect her to direct proceedings now; she was the nurse.

'Let me get dressed, and if you can get me a towel I'll use that to support Edward's neck. Leave him in his pyjamas, there's no need for him to get changed.' The less Edward moved around the better, as far as Maggie was concerned.

Within ten minutes they had carried Ed to the car and were on their way. Maggie had fashioned a cervical collar from the bath towel and she sat with Edward in the back, helping to support his head, while Juliet drove to the clinic. Ben had phoned ahead and the radiographer was expecting them. She had a wheelchair waiting for Ed and whisked him straight into X-ray, with Juliet following, leaving Maggie in the waiting area, pacing the floor, unable to settle.

She counted the squares in the linoleum, a small grey-and-white chequerboard pattern. Five squares to a pace, five paces across the room; twenty-five squares there, another twenty-five back. As she turned for the seventh trip, after one hundred and fifty squares, Ben arrived.

He stopped just inside the door and Maggie ceased her pacing. The room shrank until it felt as though they were the only two in the space.

He was wearing jeans, a black T-shirt and a black leather jacket, and she had never seen anyone look better. He looked capable, strong and comfortable—all the things she wanted to be.

He also looked far hotter than anyone should look at this hour on a Sunday morning. He looked as if he'd just rolled out of bed, which she knew was the case, and she felt a pang of unexpected jealousy as she wondered whether anyone had shared his bed.

His eyes met hers and she felt the pull, the irresistible magnetic force that joined her to him. Suddenly it didn't matter if he'd had company; he was here now, with her.

'Any news?' he asked as he crossed the floor and came to her side.

'No, they've just gone through.'

'I'm sure he's fine. There was nothing to indicate any problems yesterday.'

Maggie knew that was true but that didn't stop her from worrying, although Ben's words were spoken so calmly and confidently that she almost believed him. How had he guessed how worried she was? Was she that transparent or was he just able to read people well? And how had she come to rely on him for reassurance so quickly?

'I know, but there's a part of me that can't relax.'

Ben looked at her, his turquoise eyes studying her carefully, and she felt he could read her thoughts. 'It's OK.'

'You must think I'm a complete nervous Nellie. First Edward's accident yesterday and now, panicking over a stiff neck.'

'It's no problem. Between Juliet's medical history and now Ed you've had a lot happening. It's understandable if you're on edge. Most people would be.'

'There's more to it than that. I'd like to explain if you'd like to hear?' Maggie felt she owed him an explanation. Maybe he didn't need to hear it—he certainly seemed to be in tune with her and could probably guess why she was so paranoid—but she wanted to offer him something in return for the consolation and comfort he was giving her.

Ben nodded. 'Wait here, I'll be right back,' he said as he sat her gently in a chair beside the door. He went to the desk and spoke briefly to the clerk before returning to Maggie. He took her hand. 'Let's get some fresh air. The receptionist will ring me when Juliet comes out.' Ben guided her outside, out of earshot of everyone else in the waiting room, and it was only then that Maggie became aware that other people had arrived at the clinic.

'Would you like to walk or sit?' There was a bench just outside the clinic door but across the road was a small park.

'Let's walk,' she said, knowing she'd find it easier to launch in to her story if she were moving. She wasn't normally this forthcoming with stories about herself but she found she wanted to tell Ben, wanted to explain to him, wanted him to understand. But she wasn't brave enough to sit still and tell him; she wasn't brave enough to keep eye contact. He could already read her too well, and she didn't want him deducing things she wasn't ready to talk about.

They crossed the road, entering the park through a pair of old iron gates. The park was empty at this hour of the morning and as they walked along the winding gravel path she began to talk. 'I never used to be quite so nervous about things. As a nurse you get desensitised to a lot of things, but when something affects you personally, that's different.' The path they took was in sunlight, but the sun was weak at this time of the year and the air was cool. Maggie tied her jacket more tightly to keep the breeze out. 'I need to tell you about my husband. Steven was a policeman. Most of the time that didn't bother me. A lot of their work isn't dangerous—usually it's pretty routine, sometimes even downright boring—but every now and then there'd be something that was a little out of the ordinary, something that did put them at risk. But Steven always managed to come through unscathed and, while I worried, I never thought anything really serious would happen.'

The path narrowed slightly and she stepped closer to Ben. She was conscious of his arm brushing against hers, their steps in sync.

'But one day things changed. It was the summer holidays and Sydney was sweltering in the middle of a heat wave. Tempers were fraying and general violence was escalating among tired, bored, uncomfortable Sydneysiders. One day a fight broke out at the beach between two different ethnic groups, and the police were called in to break it up. The beach was part of Steven's beat.

'It was quite brutal and the situation got very ugly very quickly. There were men with knives and those without were using anything they could lay their hands on as weapons—breaking wooden slats off benches, hurling rubbish bins, chairs and empty bottles. Steven, of course, was right in amongst it, all the police were. At some point Steven hit his head. He couldn't remember if he'd been hit with something and had then fallen or whether he'd fallen after being pushed or even if he'd just tripped, and naturally, no one had seen anything.

'He had a big lump on the back of his head but initially he said he was fine. He'd been taken to hospital and discharged home but by night time he was complaining of a headache. He took some painkillers and went to bed but the headache got worse. He woke me up during the night, saying he'd never felt such bad pain before.'

The path meandered under a large Moreton Bay fig tree that blocked the pale sunlight. Maggie shivered and Ben wrapped his left arm around her shoulders and rubbed her arm. Maggie wasn't sure whether his gesture was intended to comfort her or simply to warm her but either way it helped ease the pain of this memory. She leant against him and continued to talk. 'His left pupil was dilated and fixed—earlier it had been fine—so I took him back to the emergency department. Being a police officer he didn't wait—the doctors saw him immediately. A CT scan showed a blood clot in his brain. It was after midnight by now and the neurosurgeon had to be called in. The clot dislodged before he got there.' She took a deep breath, steeling herself for the next sentence. 'Steven didn't make it.'

Ben stopped walking then and turned her towards him, pulling her tight against his chest. He felt warm and safe, and she could have happily stayed there all day but she hadn't finished her story yet. She lifted her head, pulling her chest away just a fraction but not enough to break the circle of his arms. 'So now, whenever someone hits their head, even in a minor way, I have a tendency to panic. I know I do but I can't help it. I know how easily it can happen. That's why I froze when Ed hit his head—the worst-case scenario always springs to mind now.'

A strand of hair had fallen across her cheek. Ben lifted one hand and tucked it behind her ear, his fingers grazing her face. 'Why didn't you insist on a scan for Edward yesterday? Would that have helped?'

Maggie's heart was pounding. She always found this topic highly emotional, and Ben's touch was sending her hormones into overdrive, stirring her emotions even further. She was surprised to find she could still speak. 'I know I panic and I've tried to teach myself to be logical. Not every bump on the head is going to result in a blood clot.'

'Edward's was a bit more than a little bump.'

'I know, but you were checking his pupils, and he had no memory loss or motor dysfunction. His headache went with pain relief. There really wasn't any reason to panic but I did anyway. I was awake most of the night checking him. I ended up sleeping in his room so I'd hear if he called out, and when he couldn't move his neck this morning I started to worry all over again.'

'You had perfectly good reasons to worry. I'd worry too if I'd lived your story, but I'm sure he's fine.' If he had anything further to add he was distracted as his phone beeped in his pocket. Ben retrieved it. 'OK, thanks. We're on our way.' He closed his phone.

'Is everything OK?'

'Seems to be. They've just finished with the doctor.'

Maggie spun around and headed back to the Sports Medicine Clinic with Ben matching her stride.

'So any other phobias I need to know about?' he asked her. 'Spiders, fear of flying, anything like that?'

'I do have some bravado,' she replied, nudging him with her elbow as he held the door for her.

Juliet and Edward were in the waiting room when Ben and Maggie returned. Ed had a cervical collar around his neck and the sight of him made Maggie stop in her tracks and she felt her shoulders tense with worry. All OK, Ben had said! But why was Edward in a neck brace?

Maggie felt Ben's arm around her again, and his reassuring touch calmed her nerves a bit.

'Come on, look at the big grin on his face. I reckon he's OK,' he said.

Maggie noticed then that her nephew was smiling. Ben was right—he didn't look like a kid with serious injuries.

Juliet was watching them, and Maggie saw her register Ben's arm around her shoulders. Her sister's knowing smirk was enough to mobilise her. She stepped forward, out of Ben's embrace, determined to stay in control of her emotions this time.

'What did the X-rays show?' she asked.

Juliet stood as she answered. 'Nothing. He's been seen by the radiologist and the orthopod, and they think it's just severe muscle spasm. There doesn't appear to be any bone damage, no fractures in the neck or skull and no sign of any internal bleeding. The orthopod doesn't think there's any underlying damage. He says it's probably just a result of yesterday's trauma.' She was stroking Edward's head as she spoke. 'He's given him some mild muscle relaxants and wants him to wear the brace to support his head and hopefully give his neck muscles a chance to relax.'

'So he's been given the all-clear? He can come home?'

Juliet nodded. 'He'll be off school for a day or two and he has a physio appointment for tomorrow but the doctor expects it all to settle fairly quickly.'

'But what if my black eyes are gone by the time I go back to school?' Edward asked.

Juliet rolled her eyes and looked at Maggie and grinned. 'If you need any more proof that he's fine, there it is!' She turned to her son. 'I'm sure you'll still be able to see some of the bruises and I'll take a photo of you just in case, OK?'

'Good news, then,' said Ben.

'Yes,' Juliet replied, adding, 'thank you for staying—you didn't need to.'

'I thought Maggie could use the company.'

Juliet raised an eyebrow and looked questioningly at Maggie. Fortunately Ben had turned to face her too and missed Juliet's look. Maggie kept quiet.

'I'll call you later to make sure all your patients are OK,' Ben said to her, 'but ring me before then if you're worried about anything. Doesn't matter what it is.'

He squeezed her shoulder before he left, raising a hand in farewell to Edward and Juliet. 'Go home and rest, both of you,' he said, directing his comment to Juliet. 'Doctor's orders.'

'Yes, sir!' Juliet replied as Maggie wondered how long it would take before the questions would begin.

It took longer than she expected.

They were in the car and Maggie was driving before Juliet started her cross-examination. Had she waited until she had a captive audience? Maggie remembered using the same tactic on her kids when they were teenagers. If you talked to them while they were in the car you didn't need to keep eye contact, so they felt more comfortable but they couldn't get away!

'So what did you two do while you were waiting?'

'We went for a walk in the park.'

'And?'

'And what?' Maggie stalled for time.

'What did you do there?'

Maggie shrugged. 'Nothing. We talked.'

'What about?' Juliet asked. Maggie kept her eyes fixed on the road ahead and kept her lips closed. 'You know I'll drag it out of you eventually. You might as well just tell me,' her sister added.

Maggie sighed. 'Steven.'

'What! You told him about Steven?'

Maggie knew why Juliet was so surprised. She didn't talk about Steven to anyone who hadn't known him. It was her story and hers alone. She still couldn't explain why she felt it was important for Ben to know. She certainly didn't have to tell him as much as she had, although she still hadn't told him everything.

'Technically, *I* didn't tell him about Steven, you did.'

'Me?' Juliet was frowning. 'When?'

'In Theatre. You mentioned Steven when they were resuscitating you. Ben thought you were talking to him until I explained who Steven was.'

'How much does he know?'

'Most of it.' Even with her gaze focused on the road Maggie could feel Juliet's raised eyebrows.

'You didn't see me when Ed hit his head. I wanted Ben to understand why I freaked out over the accident,' she explained.

'Wow. He must really be something.'

Maggie shrugged her shoulders. 'I like him.'

Juliet laughed. 'That's pretty obvious. What is it that you like exactly?'

'He's pretty easy on the eyes,' Maggie said with a smile. 'But I like the way he makes me feel. When I'm with him I don't feel like a skinny forty-two-year-old with small boobs and a bump in my nose. I feel feminine and desirable. I feel special. And he's easy to talk to. He's a good listener but it's more than that. Most of the time he just gets me. He seems to know me. There are no preconceptions like there are with people in Sydney. To him, I'm just Maggie. I'm not someone's widow or someone's mother. He doesn't know me through work or through the kids. He's not a girlfriend's ex-husband who's either trying to hit on me or terrified I'll hit on him and make things difficult with his ex.' She shrugged again. 'He's good company.'

And, although she didn't say it, when she was with Ben she didn't feel alone any more.

Which probably explained why, when Ben phoned later that day as promised and invited her again to have dinner with him, she agreed. Edward was recovering well and Maggie's concerns were dissipating. Dinner with Ben was immensely appealing.

CHAPTER FIVE

BELLA'S Restaurant was tiny and intimate, and Maggie felt enormously conspicuous as she walked in with Ben and discovered he was a regular patron. Marco and his wife, Isabella, were perfect hosts and obviously knew him well. They greeted him by name and also with a kiss on both cheeks, European style. Maggie smiled at the picture of Ben almost bending himself in half so the two Italians could reach him. They were polite and welcoming to Maggie also but she couldn't help but wonder how she compared to Ben's past companions.

The restaurant was on Lygon Street, a street renowned for its cafés and restaurants, but Bella's was already almost full. The dining room was wider than it was deep and divided down the centre by a bar. Three large, communal dining tables filled one side of the room, and there were seven smaller tables on the other side, seating two to four guests each. Marco showed Ben and Maggie to a table set for two in the window.

Ben held her chair for her, and she ran her eyes over him again as she lowered herself into her seat. He looked fabulous. He was wearing dark jeans and a pale grey shirt that made his eyes look more grey than blue. Smouldering.

Maggie was wearing a pale pink top—a colour she knew suited her—but now, amongst the trendily dressed European-looking crowd, she felt decidedly out of place. She fidgeted with her neckline.

'Are you too hot?' Ben asked.

'No. Just wishing I'd worn something else. Something black.'

Ben laughed. 'I'm glad you didn't. Melbournians seem to all wear black. You have no idea how nice it is to see something different. And that colour suits you.'

Suddenly it didn't matter what she was wearing—Ben thought she looked good.

'Thank you.' She smiled at him, her confidence restored. 'Do you always know the right thing to say?'

'I'd like to think so—years of practice, you see.' He winked at her and Maggie didn't doubt he'd had just that—years of practice. She wondered what else he'd learnt.

'Do tell.' She said but as the words left her mouth she wondered if she was actually game to hear.

'What would you like to know?'

Where did she start?

He must have thought she was never going to answer because he said, 'Why don't I get us a drink from the bar while you think of what you want to know most? Shall I order you a glass of pinot grigio?'

'That would be lovely, thanks.' As Ben moved to the bar Maggie realised she wanted to know everything. How old was he? How many siblings did he have? Why had he become a doctor? Had he been married? Why didn't he have children? What was his favourite movie?

But which of these questions was appropriate for a first date?

When he returned with their drinks she went with, 'What made you choose plastic surgery as your specialty?'

'It's plastic and reconstructive surgery technically,' he said with a grin as he took his seat opposite her. 'Haven't you looked me up on the internet?'

'No.' Was he serious? 'I never even thought of it. Are you that important that I'd find you on the web.'

'Apparently.'

'My kids would look you up, I'd rather have a conversation. Call me old-fashioned but I wouldn't even know where to start.'

'An old-fashioned girl—that's something you don't find every day.' Ben smiled at her and Maggie immediately relaxed, knowing instinctively that he didn't think old-fashioned meant boring. 'Let me order and then you can ask me anything you like. Do you want to choose something or do you trust me?'

'I trust you to order.'

Ben called Marco over to the table. 'We'll have the mushroom ravioli and the gnocchi followed by veal scaloppine and linguine marinara. Thanks, Marco.'

'That sounds like a lot of food.'

'You won't be sorry. Isabella is the best cook

I know, and don't think I haven't noticed your caveat on trusting me.'

'What do you mean?'

'You said you trust me to order—do I take it you don't trust me on other things?'

'You make me nervous,' she admitted.

'Really?' Ben's raised eyebrows suggested that wasn't the reply he'd expected.

'I'm not sure why you invited me to dinner.' There, that was the big question she'd wanted to know the answer to since the start of the evening.

'You want to know what my motives are?'

'Something like that.'

He paused and Maggie's nerves returned as she wondered what his answer would be. 'You never say what I expect you to say—I find that intriguing. I find *you* intriguing,' he answered.

'Me?'

'Yes. You wouldn't believe how refreshing it is to meet someone who isn't afraid to have a proper conversation. Or should I say, who knows *how* to have a proper conversation. And I think you've had a very interesting life. The circle I move in is very small. I've known many of the people for years, and the women spend most of their time talking about the latest club, the best tanning salon and their next vacation spot.'

'There must be *some* interesting women?'

'Most definitely. But they're all married and most of them won't have dinner on their own with me.'

'So I'm not the only one who doesn't trust your motives?' she joked as she sipped her wine.

He laughed and held up a hand in mock protest. 'I promise I've never made a move on a married woman.' He paused. 'Not deliberately anyway.'

Marco delivered their entrées and Ben placed the ravioli in front of Maggie. She waited until he'd started on his gnocchi before asking her next question, using her meal as an excuse to avoid looking at him as she nosed her way into his private life. 'Have you ever been married?'

If Ben was surprised by the question he didn't show it. He shook his head as he swallowed his food. 'No. I'm not the settling-down sort. I don't want children so there's no point really.'

'You don't want children?'

'No, I'm a career person.'

Maggie couldn't believe it; having seen him interact with both Rory and Edward in vastly different situations she couldn't imagine him not wanting a family of his own. She raised her eyebrows, silently asking him to elaborate.

'Believe me, I know how much time and effort it takes to raise a family—I see that with Rory—and I don't think I can do justice to children and my career. I don't think there are enough hours in the day. I travel a lot and I've seen things that aren't right—children suffering from sickness, war, hunger—and I don't think raising a family is for me.'

Maggie remembered all the African art. 'The photos in your office, did you take those?'

Ben nodded. 'I travelled to Uganda last year to work in a hospital there, doing reconstructive work. It was an amazing experience, confrontational at times but also immensely rewarding.'

'How long where you there?'

'Eight weeks. I'm going again in a few weeks' time, once I've raised a bit more money.'

'You pay to work there?' she asked.

'Not exactly but I don't get any financial benefit from that work. Some of my income here goes towards equipment, medical supplies, that sort of thing, but there's a lot of fund-raising as well to pay for nurses, drugs, hospital administration, general expenses. Most of my surgeries in Uganda aren't life-or-death situations but rather reconstructive, to improve patients' quality of life. They can't afford to pay for it so I have to work out ways to fund everything. To be fair, my family's foundation contributes a lot financially towards my hobby.'

'It sounds like more than a hobby.' She wondered if he'd notice she didn't question him about the foundation. Would that give her away—tell him she knew more about him than she was letting on? She decided she couldn't be bothered about that, not when he was divulging other such personal information.

'Yes, it's my dream, to be honest, and finally getting there last year was a culmination of years of work.'

'What made you choose to work there?' As someone who had only experienced health care in a first-world country she found the subject fascinating.

'My sister and I were brought up to believe that having money doesn't make you a better person—it's what you do with that money. And in Africa the work of one person can make an enormous difference. To me, it's an incredible feeling to be able to help people, children, who are disfigured, some through war and others with congenital defects. Africa and her people have really got under my skin. Most of these people have nothing, so to be able to give them something, to help to give them a better life, is such a privilege. Africa is an amazing place. Have you ever been there?'

'I've never been overseas. I was a child bride, remember—babies followed soon after, and then, as a single mother, overseas holidays weren't really on the agenda.'

'What about now? Do you have a desire to travel?'

Maggie sensed he wanted to change the topic, steer it away from himself. She could oblige even though she wanted to hear more about Ben's dreams. 'I've always wanted to see Paris.'

'What's stopping you?'

'Now you *sound* like a man who doesn't have a wife and children. It's not that easy to sneak off. There always seems to be someone who needs me.'

'Is that how you see it? Sneaking off?'

Maggie shrugged. 'I guess I must. Obviously my priority isn't getting away,' she said with a smile.

'Maybe it's time you did something for yourself.'

'I am. Having dinner with you is the most selfish thing I've done with my time in a long while.'

'I better make it worth it, then.'

Ben looked at her with such intensity it was all she could do to stop herself from reaching out to touch him. A warm glow spread through her which she recognised as desire. She hadn't felt that good in a long time. 'It already is.' Goodness, how forward she sounded—where had that come from?

She was so comfortable with Ben's company. The conversation was easy, and it felt as though they were the only two in the room. Immersed in their own little world the conversation didn't lapse into any uncomfortable silences as Maggie found herself falling under Ben's spell.

She'd started the evening thinking he was charming, intelligent and handsome. By the time they'd eaten their main courses she was adding generous, considerate and thoughtful to Ben's list of attributes.

There had to be something wrong with him. He didn't want commitment, that was obvious, but even his lack of desire to have children couldn't be seen as a negative. He had valid reasons for that decision, and while she couldn't imagine not having her own children she knew that not everyone shared her point of view.

Eventually they were the only two remaining in the restaurant.

'Do you think Marco and Isabella would like us to go home now?' Maggie asked, reluctant to end the evening but knowing it couldn't last forever.

Ben looked around the restaurant, and Maggie

could swear he hadn't noticed that all the other patrons had gone. Had he been as engrossed in her company as she was in his? Could she dare to think that?

'I'm like family to them but perhaps we'd better go before I get asked to help with the dishes.' He laughed.

She added down-to-earth to her list which, at the beginning of the night, would have surprised her given his family tree but now, after listening to his story, she could see how that was possible.

Ben went to pay their bill and thank Marco and Isabella before returning to help her up from her chair. Marco and Isabella came with him to farewell them both, kissing Maggie on both cheeks too now, and she was touched to be included in their ritual.

She left the restaurant on a high, and when Ben took her hand as they walked along Lygon Street she didn't hesitate or resist. It just felt right.

It wasn't late, still well before midnight, and there were plenty of people wandering along the footpaths or sitting having coffee at the sidewalk tables, sheltered from the chill of the evening by clear café blinds and warmed by the outdoor gas heaters.

Ben pointed out the landmarks from a recent television drama that had been filmed in and around Melbourne. Lygon Street had featured frequently as the site of the meeting places of the real-life 'underworld' figures on whom the telemovie had been based. The drama had been a huge ratings success with its, mostly, accurate storylines of sex, drugs, money and violence— stories people would never have believed if they hadn't been based on real events.

Ben and Maggie had walked less than two blocks when a loud explosion split the air. Maggie jumped, frightened by the unexpected noise. Ben's stories and the sound combined to conjure up threatening images, and she imagined a gun being fired. She paused in her tracks.

A second explosion followed the first and a faint scent of gunpowder carried to them on the evening breeze.

'What was that?' she asked as she moved

slightly closer to Ben, pressing against his side, taking comfort in his bulk.

'It's OK, I think it's just firecrackers,' he replied, seeming nonplussed.

Maggie breathed out and moved forward again, walking with Ben. As they reached an intersection a crowd of young men surged around the corner. They surrounded the two of them, separating Maggie from Ben. Maggie was jostled and bumped. The men smelt of beer and cigarettes. They were loud and rough.

Maggie crossed her arms over her chest, tucking her bag against her, and searched frantically for Ben. The crowd continued to swarm around her. There were too many people to fit on the sidewalk, and they overflowed onto the street and brought traffic to a standstill. Their voices were raised, yelling and shouting. Unfriendly voices which reverberated through Maggie.

She tried to push across the flow of the crowd, tried to get out of the stream of people, but it was impossible to break through. She felt herself starting to get swept along, carried back down Lygon Street towards Bella's Restaurant. She couldn't control her direction; she was at the mercy of the crowd. She tried to call out for Ben but her voice got stuck in her throat. She started to shake; she was struggling for air. She was more than afraid…. She was terrified.

Where was Ben? How could she lose sight of someone as big and tall as him?

Two men were arguing as they walked in front of her, swearing at each other, tempers building. One man pushed the other, deliberately provoking him. Maggie didn't want to be here, caught in the middle of this anger, alone.

The second man retaliated, pushing back against the first. Both of them stopped in their tracks, blocking her path. The first man threw a punch as the crowd behind her continued to push forwards. Maggie was trapped and in a moment she'd be in the middle of the brawl herself.

She felt someone's arms grabbing her from behind. She found her voice; she screamed and struggled, fighting against the hold.

'Maggie, it's me, Ben. It's OK, I've got you.'

His voice washed over her. She stopped struggling and instead relaxed into his hold. She was safe. He'd found her.

She felt him pick her up as if she weighed no more than a child. His arms were wrapped around her as he carried her away from the crowd. The masses parted for Ben as he moved forwards across the footpath towards the buildings. For her the mass of bodies had been impenetrable but now it was as if Ben was Moses parting the Red Sea.

He reached a doorway and gently stood Maggie down. Her knees were shaking so badly Ben was unable to let her go completely. If he had she would have collapsed in a quivering mess at his feet. He held her, shielding her from the crowd.

'You're safe. We're back at Bella's,' he said.

Maggie recognised the restaurant through the window; they were standing in the doorway. Ben reached over her shoulder and pushed the door. It swung open and he ushered her inside. He called out to Marco, letting him know they were back before locking the door.

'What's happened?' Marco asked as he emerged from the kitchen.

'We got caught up in the middle of some soccer fans. Unfortunately they weren't all barracking for the same team and things got a little out of control.'

Marco glanced out the window where hoards of people continued to stream past. 'No matter. You wait here for as long as you like—we're just cleaning up.'

'Why don't we help you in the kitchen?' Maggie offered.

Ben saw Marco register Maggie's ashen face and the slight wobble in her voice. 'No, no, you sit here—' Marco indicated a table at the back of the room '—and I'll bring you a coffee. Maybe some grappa too.'

Marco disappeared into the kitchen. Maggie still looked visibly distressed and she moved away from the large front windows towards the table Marco had indicated. She slid onto the couch that ran along the back wall of the restaurant and served as a seat. Ben waited, taking the coffee from Marco, before sitting next to Maggie on the small couch.

Ben was confident they were in no danger but Maggie still seemed quite nervous and she jumped when someone thudded into the window. He put one hand on her thigh, surprised to find she was trembling.

'Hey, it's OK, you're safe here.'

'I hate big crowds. I'm never quite sure what's going to happen but I always expect the worst.'

Ben moved his hand from her thigh and put it around her shoulders, pulling her in close. 'I don't think we're in any danger in here. We'll stay put until everything's calmed down,' he said, attempting to reassure her.

She nodded and Ben watched her as she picked up her coffee cup; her hand was shaking so badly she spilt her coffee.

'Sorry,' she said as she grabbed a serviette and started to mop up the mess she'd made.

Ben took the serviette from her and wiped up the coffee as Marco came over and poured them each a glass of grappa. 'Here, drink this instead while your coffee cools down,' he said, passing her a glass.

Maggie's hand was still shaking as she held the glass so Ben covered her hand with his, helping her to hold the glass to her lips as she

drank. She finished the small glass in a couple
of mouthfuls and it seemed to do the trick. She
relaxed.

'Is that better?' he asked.

She nodded. His left arm was still around her
shoulders, and as she looked up at him their
faces were only inches apart. Her blue eyes
were enormous in her pale face, her freckles
clearly visible across the bridge of her nose.

He could see her breasts rising and falling with each breath, could feel them pushing against his chest as she remained tucked
against his side. Their gazes were locked, neither one aware of what was happening outside
the restaurant any longer. Both of them were
immersed in the small, imaginary bubble that
was just big enough for the two of them.

Maggie's pupils were dilated, her breathing
rapid. He could feel her breath on the side of
his neck. Her tongue darted out as she licked
her lips, giving Ben a brief glimpse of dark
pink between small white teeth. He couldn't
resist—he had to know what Maggie's lips
would feel like, what she would taste like. He
closed his eyes as he bent his head, capturing

her mouth with his, feeling her lips under his. He hadn't stopped to think, hadn't been able to think.

Her lips were soft and tasted like grappa. She smelt of orange blossom.

Her lips opened; her tongue met his, joining him in the kiss.

He cupped her face, holding her close to him, deepening the kiss. Maggie moaned and he felt her hands slide around behind his head, sending shivers of anticipation down his spine as her fingers brushed the nape of his neck.

Her lips moved under his as she nipped at his lip with her teeth, pulling his lip into her mouth. She pressed closer to him, removing a hand from behind his head and running it down his chest, leaving a trail of heat in her wake.

Her hand was on his thigh now, and it was all he could do to retain some sense of composure. He was consumed with desire; he had to regain control.

He pulled back. They were both breathing in short, rapid bursts, their hearts beating with a staccato rhythm. Her left hand was still resting on his thigh. He covered it with his and felt the warm band of metal under his fingers.

Her wedding ring.

She must have felt his fingers connect with the band and she looked down.

He expected her to move away. She didn't but she did remove her hand.

What had he been thinking? What was *she* thinking? he wondered.

He felt a brief pang of guilt—had he taken advantage of her in her distressed state? He started to apologise. 'Maggie…'

She put her hand on his chest, stopping his apology. 'Don't. It's OK, I needed a distraction.' She smiled, her blue eyes sparkling. She was relaxed, happy even.

The guilty feeling vanished when he remembered she'd kissed him back, and he knew he'd kiss her again if he had another opportunity.

'You're sure you're OK?' Ben was puzzled. He'd thought Maggie was close to going into shock and now she'd bounced back?

She nodded. 'Yes, I am now, but I'm glad you found me when you did. I don't think I would have coped much longer.'

'I'm sorry it took me that long to reach you. I could see you but I couldn't get through.'

She shook her head, her chestnut hair grazing her shoulders. 'It's not your fault.' She paused. 'I actually didn't tell you everything this morning. I have a bit of a problem with crowds as well.' He thought she was going to leave the conversation there but she continued. 'I was at the beach the day the brawl broke out, the day Steven died.' Her voice faltered. 'He wasn't supposed to be working. We'd gone to the beach for a family outing with the kids but when the fight started Steven took us to the police station. His station. He got us to safety but then he went out, joining his mates, trying to diffuse things. He got us to safety but not before I'd seen things I'd rather forget.' That explained her vivid description of the day, Ben realised. Maggie had been part of it. 'That was the day my life changed, and I've never been able to handle volatile situations since then.'

That explained a lot. Under the circumstances Ben was amazed she'd held it together for as long as she had today.

'Maggie, I'm so sorry I put you in that situation.'

'You weren't to know.'

'No, but it hasn't been a great weekend for you on a scale of one to ten, has it?'

'It hasn't been all bad,' she said with a smile.

He grinned back at her. She really was an amazing woman. He was constantly surprised by people's resilience. He'd seen it many times in his patients, but for Maggie to not only get through tonight but to be able to finish the evening with a smile on her face was incredible. He wanted to work out what made her tick. He wanted to kiss her again but he'd have to choose the right moment. It wasn't now.

The street was silent again; the crowd had moved on. It was time to leave the sanctuary of the restaurant. 'I'll fetch the car and bring it back here to collect you.' He didn't want to risk taking Maggie back out into the neighbourhood.

Maggie didn't bother arguing. She wasn't keen on braving the streets again, and if Ben was prepared to fetch the car she was prepared to wait, pleased to have a chance to reflect on what had just transpired between them. 'Thank you.'

'My pleasure. I'll just let Marco know.' Ben stood but not before he gave her another light kiss on the lips, a much gentler, softer kiss but one that she still felt burn through her body from her lips to her toes. Her stomach was tumbling with desire and her legs were like jelly. Maggie knew her legs wouldn't be able to support her for some time and that had nothing to do with the earlier crowds and everything to do with Ben. She sank back into the couch, pleased to have a chance to collect her thoughts.

Ben left via the front door, and as she watched him go she decided to add sexy to her list of attributes for him and then wondered if she shouldn't add dangerous as well. Now she knew what the expression 'to be swept off your feet' meant. With Steven it hadn't really been a case of being swept off her feet. They'd practically grown up together at high school, and she'd always known they belonged together but she couldn't remember ever experiencing such a strong and unexpected rush of desire.

She pushed Steven to the back of her mind. She'd made a conscious decision to have dinner with Ben and she certainly hadn't resisted his kiss. Now was not the time for thoughts of the past.

She fiddled with her wedding ring, twisting it around her finger. She'd never taken it off, not because she still felt married but because there'd never been any need to. She had no idea where things were headed with Ben but for the first time she wondered if there would come a day when she might want to remove her wedding ring.

A shadow fell across the table, and she looked up to see Marco standing beside her.

'Do you mind if I join you?' he asked.

'Of course not,' she said as Marco pulled out a chair opposite her.

'He is a nice man, no?'

'Very nice,' Maggie agreed with a smile, thinking she'd just come to the same conclusion. Marco and his wife were obviously very fond of Ben, and she was intrigued by their relationship. 'How is it that you know him?'

'Ahh, he operated on our grandson. He was

born with a cleft palate. My daughter was so upset but Ben fixed it. *Perfecto.*' Marco emphasised his point by putting his thumb and forefinger together in a circle before raising them to his lips and kissing them with a flourish. 'He is lovely man. And now,' he said with a shrug, 'he is family. He eats with us often and it's always good to see him. We owe him a huge debt.'

As Marco finished speaking Ben pulled his car into the curb.

'Ah, here he is.' Marco stood, waiting for Maggie to stand as well. 'It was lovely to meet such a beautiful lady. We hope to see you again soon,' he said as he took Maggie's hands in his and kissed her again on both cheeks before accompanying her to the door where Ben was waiting.

'Beware of this man, Maggie,' Ben said, winking at her as he held the door open. 'Casanova was an Italian, remember.' Maggie just beamed, happier than she could remember being for some time.

'The ladies didn't complain, Ben. Casanova must have done something right.' Marco managed to get the last word in as Ben closed the door for Maggie.

The trip home was quiet as Maggie reflected on the night's events. She took a deep breath, surprised to find she felt remarkably calm. Her heart rate was back to normal. No thanks to Ben.

She was still stunned by the intensity of her feelings, the response he was able to evoke from her. Where had that come from? She'd completely lost herself in his kiss; time and place had no meaning.

What had she been thinking?

She knew she hadn't been thinking—she hadn't been capable of thinking. Only feeling. When his fingers had felt her wedding ring she realised then that wearing the ring was a habit; she was used to it being on her finger. Her reaction to Ben's kisses certainly hadn't been one of a woman who still felt married.

She lay in bed later, replaying the evening in her mind.

When she was caught in the crowd, trapped and terrified, she thought that feeling would haunt her for a long time, but Ben's kiss had eradicated everything else from her mind. How was that possible? He'd rescued her from the crowd, carried her to safety and then wiped all memory of that event with his kiss. Almost all she could recall from the evening was the feel of his hand on her face, his fingers on her cheek and the first touch of his lips on hers, the sweet taste of his mouth. He'd set her senses on fire.

Ben had kissed her again when he pulled up in front of Juliet's house. Or did she kiss him? She'd had no idea she could be so forward but she didn't doubt that she'd been as much the instigator of another kiss. There had been no discussion, yet somehow they were kissing again, making out in the car like a couple of teenagers.

Ben's kisses had transported her to a different place, a world away from her everyday life, and once she'd tasted him she couldn't get enough. She was like a hummingbird drawn to the sweet smell of nectar and she knew she could easily become addicted. She tried to remember how she'd felt when Steven had kissed her. They'd been so young and inexperienced when they first got together. She laughed—she was still inexperienced. It wasn't as if she had a lot of notches in the bed post.

She lay with her left hand on her chest as she twisted her wedding ring around on her finger. What would Steven think of Ben?

For the first time Maggie realised that it didn't matter what Steven would have thought. Her life was her own now. The kids were adults, living their own lives; she was entitled to live hers. And as Juliet said, she was entitled to have some fun.

So that was exactly what she planned to do.

The next five days went past in the blink of an eye. Maggie knew it was because she was busy but by Friday all she could remember about the week were the moments which had included Ben. He had phoned the house several times to check on Edward's progress and had called in unexpectedly after work one evening. He'd said it was to check on his young patient but he'd invited Maggie to a movie and she accepted. Juliet had all but pushed her out the door.

Maggie knew she was floating on air but Ben

was such good company. She could scarcely wait until Juliet's next appointment. She'd begun to count the hours until she saw Ben again, as pathetic as that made her feel.

Finally Friday dawned and Maggie drove Juliet to her appointment, but parking spaces were scarce so she dropped Juliet at the door and then looked for an empty spot. By the time she got into the waiting room Juliet was already in with Ben. Disappointment flooded her as she realised she wouldn't see him now. There was no need for her to be in the consulting room; she'd have to sit and wait with all the other patients.

'Mrs Petersen?' Ben's receptionist called across the waiting room to Maggie. 'Dr McMahon asked for you to be sent down when you got here.'

Maggie leapt to her feet; she was going to see him after all! She almost ran down the corridor and just remembered to stop and knock on the door before she burst into the room.

'Good, you're here,' Ben said as Maggie came to a stop in the middle of the room. He was washing his hands, as calm as ever, in stark contrast to Maggie's flustered demeanour.

She tried to regain some control. 'Is everything all right?'

'Everything's fine. Juliet's skin is stretching nicely. Everything is progressing as expected. I wanted to know if you've decided to accompany me to the art exhibition tomorrow night.'

'What exhibition?' Juliet chimed in as she reappeared from behind the privacy screen, shrugging into her jacket as she walked.

'Gabby and Finn are having an exhibition of my photographs at their gallery. It opens tomorrow and I invited Maggie to come with me. She hasn't given me an answer yet.'

'*Your* photographs?'

'These are Ben's photos,' Maggie said as she gestured to the photos hanging on the walls of Ben's office.

Juliet scanned the pictures. 'Yours! Wow.'

Ben shrugged. 'It's a hobby but Gabby is kind enough to put some on display, and the proceeds go towards my medical work in Africa.'

'Do you sell a lot?'

'Surprisingly, yes.' He was so self-deprecating, a trait Maggie found totally endearing. 'Why don't you come to the opening as well?' he asked Juliet. 'Maybe then Maggie will accept my invitation.'

'I'd love to but I don't think I'd find a babysitter at such short notice. You should go though, Mags. You haven't got anything else on, have you?'

Maggie frowned at her sister. She knew jolly well Maggie had a free schedule. What would she have to do on a Saturday night?

'Great. I'll pick you up at seven. Don't wear black.' Ben smiled at her as he added the condition, and Maggie knew he was thinking of her outfit dilemma from their dinner date at Bella's. A warm glow spread through her. With three words Ben was able to make her feel as though she had his full attention even though he was in the middle of a consulting list and Juliet was in the room with them. He had enough charm for ten men, she thought as she smiled back and nodded before following Juliet out of the room.

'Why didn't you say yes straight away?' Juliet

asked as they left the building and returned to the car.

'We've been to dinner and a movie. This will be our third date.'

'Why is that a problem?'

'That's the point where it starts to get complicated. Is it going to go any further? What do we do next? If we take the next step, what does that mean?'

'You're overthinking things. Don't worry about what happens next, just have fun.'

But Maggie couldn't just continue to 'have fun.' For her the third date was always a turning point, the time when she stopped and thought about what she wanted. And, in Ben's case, she knew exactly what she wanted but she also knew that if she took the next step it would be almost impossible to get him out of her system. A third date was a big deal for her and that was why she'd hesitated.

'You're only going to an art gallery with him—you're not eloping,' Juliet continued, taking advantage of Maggie's silence to dish out more advice. She looked Maggie up and down as she unlocked the car. 'What you need is a confidence-boosting dress and a killer pair of high heels. I think we should go shopping.'

'Don't you need to go home and rest?' Maggie asked hopefully. She didn't love shopping, especially not for herself.

'Nope, I'm feeling good. I think I'm getting used to these expander sessions. Let's shop,' Juliet said as she pulled her seat belt on.

The factory outlet shops in Richmond were between Ben's East Melbourne office and Juliet's house, and after trying several different shops and many different outfits Maggie managed to pick up a gorgeous deep-purple wrap dress by a well-known designer for a fraction of the normal retail price.

She took it home and hung it on the wardrobe door, and every time she looked at it over the next twenty-four hours she vacillated between third-date nerves and excitement at seeing Ben again. She hoped the dress was going to be as confidence boosting as Juliet proclaimed.

When it finally came time to get ready Juliet and Kate both helped to dress and accessorise her. The dress hugged Maggie's figure and for once she was glad she didn't have much padding—the fabric of the dress would have emphasised every bulge. Juliet produced a wide black belt that she fixed around Maggie's waist, helping to create the illusion of curves beneath the wrap dress, and Maggie completed her outfit with a pair of black knee-high boots that Juliet had insisted she buy during their shopping spree. Unlike the dress, the boots had not been on sale and the price had nearly made Maggie's eyes pop out of her head. But she had to admit, looking at her entire ensemble, that the boots really made a statement. Juliet had been right. Maggie felt confident, feminine and sexy, and more importantly, ready to meet Ben's family.

Kate brushed Maggie's chestnut hair until it shone and begged to paint her nails. Maggie relented and chose a black nail polish from Juliet's stash, removing her boots to let her niece colour her toenails. If she was going to be a vamp, she figured she might as well embrace it wholeheartedly.

Even if no one would see her toenails?

Even so, she decided. She would know and

that knowledge would give her more confidence.

'What about your make-up?' Juliet asked as they waited for Maggie's nails to dry. 'What shall we emphasise, eyes or lips?'

Maggie had no idea what lipstick she should wear to complement a purple dress. 'Eyes, I think.'

'OK,' Juliet said as she got to work adding eye make-up and blush to Maggie's base of foundation. 'You can do your lips now. I promised the kids dessert—I'd better go and do that,' Juliet said when she finished.

Maggie applied a pale lipgloss, something that wouldn't clash with her dress, and sat down to put her boots back on. As she zipped them up her wedding ring caught her eye. She slid it off her finger and looked at the white line marking where it had sat for twenty-two years.

She held the ring in her right hand, the metal pressing into her palm. Should she leave it off? Could she?

She sat on the bed and stared at her left hand. It didn't look like hers any more. It looked empty. She'd taken her engagement ring off years ago but now her hand was completely bare and it was a strange feeling.

She took the ring from her palm and held it between her thumb and forefinger. Was she being premature, taking it off? Should she put it back on?

She was still staring at the ring when she heard Kate's voice yelling from the hallway.

'He's here!'

Decision time.

On or off?

Adrenalin coursed through her system in anticipation of the evening ahead. She could feel every beat of her heart as though she had a miniature drum inside her chest counting the seconds until she saw Ben.

On or off?

Her hands were shaking as she put the ring into her handbag, zipping it into the inside pocket.

She wanted to be free to make her own choices as far as Ben was concerned. For the first time in twenty-two years she wanted to feel like a single woman.

Off.

CHAPTER SIX

THE exhibition was fabulous. Within half an hour of the scheduled start the gallery was packed with guests, all sipping champagne and sampling the cocktail food while they perused the artworks and chatted.

The gallery was in the beachside suburb of St Kilda. The front two rooms were large and airy and faced directly onto the street. The walls were painted white and in the daytime the rooms would be flooded with natural light spilling through the enormous floor-to-ceiling windows that also afforded the passing foot traffic good views of the artwork on display. St Kilda was a popular tourist haunt and Gabby and her husband, Finn, had dedicated one front room to Aboriginal art, leaving the other front room available for exhibitions—in this case African art, including Ben's photographs. Displayed on stands around the room were African carvings and beadwork that Ben had sourced for his sister to import.

Ben had some unofficial duties to attend to that involved making sure those guests who were likely to part with their money were given the proper amount of attention. Maggie had expected this and while he had introduced her to a number of the guests she was quite happy to move about the gallery on her own. The noise level was quite high and it was relatively easy in a group as large as this for Maggie to blend in.

She had spent some time in the African room and was amazed by the quality of Ben's photographs. In contrast to the landscapes and animal shots that adorned his office walls there were a large number of portraits on display here. Maggie wished several of the portraits could talk; she would have loved to listen to their stories.

As the crowd grew larger she wandered into one of the smaller rooms at the rear of the gallery. She had the space to herself for a little while before she felt someone enter the room behind her. She knew it was Ben—her senses immediately went on high alert whenever he was nearby, making her nerves tingle and raising goose bumps on her skin.

He came up behind her and wrapped his right arm around her waist. He whispered into her ear and his breath was warm on her cheek. 'Have I told you how gorgeous you look in purple?'

She turned her head slightly to look at him, aware as she did that their mouths were now inches apart. 'You could always tell me twice,' she replied.

'You look gorgeous.' Maggie felt herself blush. 'Purple suits you. And it's much easier to find you in a crowd if you're not wearing black.' He grinned. 'Are you hungry?' He brought his left hand around in front of her, offering her a plate piled high with nibbles. 'I brought a selection. I wasn't sure what you'd want.'

Maggie chose a prawn skewered on a stalk of lemongrass. 'You've managed to pull quite a crowd,' she said as she removed the prawn by its tail, separating it from the lemongrass.

'I don't know that I can take all the credit. Gabby and Finn work hard promoting these events, and I never underestimate the benefit

of having the McMahon Foundation associated
with it,' Ben said before popping a caviar blini
into his mouth.

'I'd better get back to the main gallery,' he
said when he finished eating. 'There'll be
people wondering where I am. Are you OK in
here or would you like to come with me?'

'I'm fine, thanks,' she said, touched by his at-
tentiveness. 'I'll have a look in the other rooms
for a bit and then come back to the front.'

'Don't be long,' he said as he leant forward
to kiss her cheek. 'I'll see you in a minute.'

Maggie had to stop herself from following
him immediately. She needed to show some
restraint even if his kiss had her shaking in
her new boots. She forced herself to wander
through the rest of the gallery before returning
to the African room. Almost instantly Finn appeared by her side with a refill for her drink.

'Thank you,' she said as he topped up her
champagne, 'but please don't feel you have
to look after me. I'm quite all right.' She felt
surprisingly comfortable wandering about on
her own, and she knew that was because each
time she would catch a glimpse of Ben as he

worked the room he'd have one eye on her and send her a wink or a smile. Just knowing he was aware of where she was made her feel confident. Confident enough to be brave in a room full of strangers. That plus the fact that either he or Finn would appear by her side at regular intervals to top up her champagne!

'I'm not doing this because I have to. I'm happy to look after you.' Finn's Irish accent was pronounced against the backdrop of Aussie twangs.

'Really? Ben didn't ask you to keep an eye on me?'

'No.' Finn paused before sending a cheeky grin her way. 'He didn't have to—Gabby got in first. She didn't want you to feel we were subjecting you to the Spanish Inquisition so she decided she'd leave you to me. She thought I'd be less threatening!'

'Well, I appreciate the attention, thank you.'

'Had to make sure you're enjoying yourself. Are you?'

'Very much.'

'And you like the art?'

'I do, but to be honest I'm having just as much fun watching the people.'

'Ahh, I could tell you a few stories about some of these people.'

'I don't doubt it.' She smiled at him. Maggie had taken an instant liking to Ben's brother-in-law. He had a quick, dry sense of humour and a laid-back charm. He was one of those people who, after spending five minutes with them, you felt as if you'd known them for years. She could easily imagine how Gabby, as a young art student studying in Paris, had been swept off her feet by the amusing Irishman. 'Could Ben tell some stories too?'

'Aye, he could. Different to mine, of course. There's a few hearts he's broken in this room.' Finn was nodding his head as he looked about the room but Maggie resisted the temptation to follow his gaze. 'Don't let that bother you. It's not from broken promises. It's just that they want more than Ben is prepared to give. That'll all change when he finds true love, you can bet on it.'

'Has he ever been in love?' The question

popped out of Maggie's mouth before she knew what she was saying.

'That's not my story to tell, I'm afraid, but if you want my opinion, he's still looking for true love—he just doesn't know it.' Maggie looked across the room towards Ben. Finn was watching her closely. 'Be patient with him.'

Was that true? Was Ben looking for true love? She supposed deep down it was true of most people. But why then hadn't Ben found it already? Was there something she didn't know?

That was a ridiculous question; there must be a hundred things she didn't know about Ben. Finn could probably give her a lot of the answers. She turned to ask him but he'd already darted away, off to chat with another guest. He had been blessed with the Irish gift of the gab, that was for sure.

Her gaze settled instead on Ben and she watched him as he worked the room. He was so incredibly sexy, moving fluidly through the crowd, charming the men and women alike. He was taller than most of the guests, and as he bent his head to listen she could see the faces of the female guests gazing adoringly up at him. Every now and again he'd touch someone lightly on the arm, and the women, young and old, would bask in the attention. To Maggie's eyes seeing their pleasure was the equivalent of watching someone win the lottery.

She expected to feel slightly jealous as she watched other women lap up his attentions but she found his charm was an incredibly powerful aphrodisiac. Plus he was still keeping an eye on her; a slight tilt of his head or a quick wink at regular intervals let her know he knew her whereabouts.

Her feet, in her new high-heeled boots, were beginning to complain so she perched on a zebra-skin ottoman in the centre of the room. She ran her hand over the fabric, hoping it was fake, then hoping that it was actually made for sitting on. Was she sitting on the artwork? She quickly checked for any sign of a description or price and was relieved to find nothing.

She looked up and saw Ben crossing the room towards her, and neither the artwork nor the furniture could possibly hold her attention then.

She loved the way he walked. It wasn't a swagger—describing it that way would make him sound conceited—but he definitely walked with confidence, with an air of someone who was used to being respected. Not for who he was but rather for what he did. He was comfortable in his own skin, and that confidence was obvious in the way he held himself. Even in a room as spacious as this one Ben looked larger than life. He was stopped several times by guests wanting to chat but those conversations were brief, and she knew he was coming for her. Her heartbeat increased its pace with every step he took towards her.

He sat beside her, his knees relaxed and apart, one thigh resting against hers.

'How are you holding up? Are you getting bored?'

She could hear the concern in his voice and allayed his fears. 'Not at all. My feet just need a rest.'

He glanced down at the floor. 'I'm not surprised in those heels.' He leant a little closer, his voice soft in her ear. 'I'd be happy to massage your feet for you later.'

Maggie smiled. 'I'd be happy to let you.' A foot massage was her idea of heaven. She looked at his hands—they were large but his fingers were delicate and seemed capable of giving a very good massage. 'Can I ask you a question?'

'Of course, but you should know I've never had any complaints about my massages.'

Maggie laughed and deliberately pushed against him, enjoying the feeling of her shoulder pressing into his arm. 'It's not about your massages. You have so many fabulous portraits on display here, why don't you have any in your office?'

'I can't have photos of people in the waiting room, it's too confronting.'

Maggie frowned. 'Why? Do you think the world should be full of perfect people?'

'People who look perfect, you mean?'

She nodded.

'No. That's exactly what I don't want.' He paused and glanced around the room. 'Tell me, which is your favourite photo?'

Maggie pointed at a black-and-white photo of an old African woman in profile. She had her head turned slightly and was watching some young children playing in the distance.

'This one.'

'Why?'

'It looks like she's looking back at her past, back at what her childhood was like, and it makes me want to know about her life, because she doesn't look sad that she's old now and those days are long gone. She looks content. I want her to tell me her story.'

'Exactly. She looks like she has a story to tell. People with lines, scars, even regrets, who've learned to live with all that, look comfortable in their skins, and that shows through in the photographs. The best ones are of people with character, and that's what I want to preserve in my patients. I want them to preserve their character. I don't want to turn them into someone else. That's why I don't have photos of people on the wall. I don't want them to say to me, "Make me look like that." I want them to look like themselves.'

'So no Pamela Anderson or Kate Winslet?'

Ben shook his head. 'I want people to be happy with how they look after I finish with them. I don't want them to be comparing themselves to anyone else. Not everyone can look like Angelina Jolie, and people shouldn't want to. But if I put photos of people on display, patients will compare themselves to those pictures. They might do it subconsciously but they'll all do it—it's human nature. If something needs fixing I'm happy for people to show me pictures they've chosen themselves. It gives me an idea of what my patients want the finished results to resemble. As long as they realise it's unlikely to be a perfect match and if it's going to look ridiculous—'

'Like Pammy's boobs on Juliet?'

'Yes, then I'll talk them out of it. But we have to start somewhere. So, they can give me a general idea as long as it's *their* idea.'

'So you want your patients to still look like themselves.'

'Yes. A person's face is the window to their soul and should be able to express the life they've led. You shouldn't be a blank canvas, nor should you aspire to look like someone else either because of who they are or just because you like the way they look. I want people to love their own face. I want to make it possible for people to live and love and express themselves without fear of ridicule or embarrassment. Most of my work is in reconstructive surgery, very little of what I do is purely cosmetic. If I have photos of beautiful people in the waiting room it reminds patients of their perceived flaws, and sometimes those flaws are what make them special. It's my job to mend deformities, for appearances' sake, or to improve quality of life, or for some other medical reasons, but I don't want people believing they need to change every little thing about themselves that might be considered less than perfect.

'So I could hang photos like this one you like but I think it's better not to have portraits at all. I don't want people to be influenced by my artwork. There's enough external influence. I want them to feel comfortable with what they're asking me to do and I want them to feel like it's their decision. I want to be able to read about a person in their face.'

She wondered about Finn's comment. About Ben looking for love and what might have happened to him in his past. What would she be able to read in Ben's face in another thirty years? What would she see in Ben's eyes?

'Sorry, that was a rather long-winded answer to your question. Are you ready to go? I think we could make an escape now.' Had he mistaken her silence for boredom? 'What shall we do next?' he asked.

'Before the foot massage, you mean?'

He grinned. 'Before that.'

'Could we get something to eat? You and Finn have been plying me with champagne all night, and I think I should have eaten a bit more.'

'I have plenty of food at my place. Can I interest you in a midnight snack?' Ben winked at her as he issued his invitation and his expression was so full of innuendo that Maggie nearly melted in a pool of desire at his feet.

She nodded, knowing she was agreeing to more than a late-night supper. He stood, holding out one hand to help her off the zebra-skin ottoman, and at the touch of his palm on hers the tingle of anticipation that had been building in her all night exploded in a dozen different directions through her body.

He pulled her to her feet and bent her elbow

so she was standing almost pressed against his chest. 'Are you sure about this?' he asked. If he hadn't been holding her she knew she couldn't have supported herself—adrenalin was racing through her body, making her knees shake. Her heart leapt against her ribs and desire thrummed in her veins.

She licked her lips; her mouth was dry, so dry she could barely speak. 'Positive.'

He kept hold of her hand as they said good-night to Gabby and Finn, and Maggie was barely aware of leaving the gallery—all she was conscious of was Ben's touch. They'd arrived in a chauffeured car, and Ben had kept it waiting, citing parking difficulties and lack of taxis as his excuse. Maggie had thought it extravagant but now she was extremely grateful she didn't have to wait in the cold night air. She was also aware, as she sank back into the soft leather seats, that having the car waiting for them meant she didn't have time to think about what she was doing. She just followed her hormones—her brain had shut down a long time ago.

The chauffeur delivered them to a converted

three-storey house in South Yarra, overlooking the river. Ben's apartment took up the entire top floor and had stunning views across the Yarra River to the city but Maggie wasn't interested in the view outside the windows.

He'd taken his jacket off as soon as they'd come inside and now he loosened his tie, letting it hang around his neck as he undid the top two buttons of his shirt. Maggie watched his fingers as he manipulated the buttons. She was tempted to reach out to touch the hollow at the base of his throat, to run her fingers along his collarbone and under his shirt.

'What can I get you? I have cheese, fruit, smoked salmon. Champagne.'

She dragged her eyes back to his face, away from the bare skin of his throat, and wondered if he'd stocked the fridge in anticipation of having company or if he was always prepared. 'I'd really like some toast with Vegemite.'

Ben laughed. 'I'm not sure how well that goes with champagne. Tell you what—if you stay the night I'll make you Vegemite toast for breakfast.'

The words fell so smoothly from his lips, and

she could feel herself falling further under his spell. Knowing he'd had plenty of practise at seducing women didn't make it any easier to resist him. And she didn't want to. She wanted to be here; she wanted to be under his spell.

He poured her a glass of champagne, and she reached for it with her left hand, but instead of handing her the drink Ben put the glass on the benchtop and took her hand in his. He turned it over. 'Where is your wedding ring?'

'I took it off.'

'Why?' He ran his thumb over the white line her ring had left on her finger. His fingers were nestled in her palm, and Maggie could barely speak because of the sparks of desire that were shooting from her palm to her chest.

'I didn't want to look like a married woman tonight. I didn't want Gabby and Finn to get the wrong idea.' She wasn't ready to tell him her real reasons, the reason she was standing here in his kitchen. She wasn't ready to tell him how she'd been imagining what his body looked like under his clothes, imagining how his hands would feel on her bare skin. What if their relationship went no further? She would have made a complete fool of herself.

Ben took a step towards her until he was standing only a few inches away. He lifted her hand, bringing it up to his mouth. 'And what would that idea have been?' he asked as he kissed her fingertips. This time the sparks of desire shot straight to her breasts. Maggie felt her nipples harden as Ben lips melted her fingers. She leaned back against the bench, needing its bulk to hold her up, and this time she really couldn't speak. Ben answered his own question. 'The idea that I wanted to bring that woman home with me and watch her drink champagne so I could taste it from her lips afterwards?'

He lowered her hand and leaned forward a fraction more. Maggie tilted her head up, expecting to be kissed, but Ben just brought his mouth to her ear and whispered, 'Have I got the general idea?'

Maggie nodded again; it was all she was capable of.

'It seems to me you're in need of a champagne, then,' he said as he reached behind her and picked up the two champagne glasses in one hand. He handed her one glass, clinking his against it in a silent toast.

Maggie sipped her champagne, deliberately maintaining eye contact and watching Ben's eyes follow the movement of her mouth, watched his lips part as his breathing deepened. He moved towards her, closing the distance, but she sidestepped him. She wanted to savour this moment; she wanted to tease him a bit more.

She took his hand and led him to the couch. Her wrap dress slipped as she took her seat, revealing one thigh. She pulled the fabric of the skirt across to cover her legs.

'Don't.' Ben reached for her hand, removing it from her lap. The fabric slipped off her leg again, and he ran his hand over her skin, grazing the inside of her thigh.

Waves of desire washed over Maggie and it took all her concentration to remember just to breathe. The touch of his fingertips on her bare skin sent a buzz of anticipation straight to her groin and she felt as though she was on fire. She closed her eyes, relishing the sensation as

Ben's touch brought her body to life. She'd forgotten who was teasing who.

She felt him remove her champagne flute from her grasp and opened her eyes to see him offer it to her for another sip before putting it on the coffee table. He leant towards her, his face inches from hers, his lips close enough to lick. He was so close she could feel her breasts brush against his shirt each time she breathed in. She parted her lips, breathing in deeply, savouring his smell. He reached for her, two fingers under her chin, tipping her face up to his. About to taste the champagne from her lips as promised.

Maggie leant back into the sofa and heard herself moan as he kissed her. Kissed her hard. She parted her lips, welcoming his tongue into her mouth. Letting him explore her and taste her as she tasted him.

He reached down and lifted her right foot, unzipping her boot and pulling it off before doing the same with the left one. He brought her legs into his lap and ran his fingers up the inside of her calf and underneath the hem of her dress, stroking her knee. He bent his head and kissed her again, the promised foot massage forgotten by them both.

His hand left her knee and teased at the neckline of her dress, and the crossover front of the wrap dress offered no resistance to his inquisitive fingers. Maggie gasped as his fingers brushed over her breast and she felt her nipple harden in expectation as his fingers slipped inside her bra. He found her nipple, stopping to tease it, running his fingers around it and over it, sending electric shocks through her body.

He loosened her belt and her dress fell open, revealing black lace underwear. He pushed the lace of her bra aside, freeing her breast. He was in control and Maggie was incapable of doing anything except succumbing to his touch. She moaned again as he ran his fingers over first one nipple, then the other.

He trailed a line of kisses down her neck to her breasts and ran his tongue across one nipple, turning Maggie dizzy with desire before he took her other breast into his mouth, sucking it and making her writhe in ecstasy. She raised her hips off the couch, unable to lie still, pushing them towards Ben.

She needed him to touch her. Needed to feel his hands on her. She couldn't think beyond where his fingers might land next. Where she might next feel his mouth on her skin. She was consumed by need. By passion.

She reached for him now, her hands reading her mind, tugging at his shirt. She pulled it free from his pants, running her fingers up inside the shirt, over his skin, feeling the heat radiating from him.

She undid his belt and her fingers fumbled with the button on his waistband. He lifted her legs from his lap and, with one hand, pushed his trousers off his hips and onto the floor. He lay beside her on the couch, one hand still between her thighs, as he moved his mouth back to cover hers, kissing her deeply.

Maggie knew where this night would end—there was no denying that, just as there was no denying she wanted it as badly as she'd wanted anything in her entire life. As far as she was concerned she was Ben's for the taking.

His hand parted her thighs and he lay one of his legs across hers, pinning her to the couch. His hand moved higher until he found the place where her legs joined, until his hand covered her most sensitive spot. A place that felt like the centre of the universe. Her universe. He slid his hand under the elastic of her underpants, and she could feel the moisture coming from her, preparing her for the next progression.

He slid one finger inside her, and Maggie closed her eyes, almost unable to bear the waves of desire crashing through her. Heat flooded through her and she was desperate to feel Ben's skin on hers. She tugged his shirt over his head until they were lying chest to chest, skin to skin. His fingers continued to work their magic; he was bringing her to a peak of pleasure. She threw her head back as she thrust her hips towards him, and just when she thought she was about to explode he paused.

She opened her eyes and she saw the question in his face. She didn't want him to stop; there was only one conclusion she could bear to have. She pushed his underpants down over his hips, freeing him, and her hand closed around his shaft. He was fully aroused, firm and warm in her hand, and as she ran her fingers up his shaft and across the sensitive tip she heard him gasp with pleasure.

She wanted him unable to resist, she wanted him at her mercy and she wanted him inside her.

She pulled his head down to her and kissed him hard, wondering at what point she had become the leader. She broke away, biting his lip gently between her teeth and making eye contact. She wanted to watch him, wanted to see his expression as she took control.

She pushed him backwards slightly, adjusting her hips before she brought him back to her and guided him inside. She welcomed him in and wrapped her legs around him to keep him close. He closed his eyes and a sigh of pleasure escaped his lips. Maggie lifted her hips, pushing him deeper inside her and closed her eyes too as she listened to him moan in delight. She concentrated on the rhythm of movement, the sensation of their bodies joined together as he thrust into her.

But he wasn't to be outdone. He found a gap between their hips and with one hand he found the source of her pleasure. His fingers moved in small, soft circles that almost brought her undone.

She heard his name on her lips as he thrust inside her, as his fingers continued their magic, bringing her to a peak of excitement.

'Now, please,' she begged for release. She couldn't hold on any longer. Her head was thrown back and Ben dropped his head to her breast, sucking on a nipple. She lifted her hands to his head, holding onto his hair, keeping his head down as he brought her to a climax. Her entire body shuddered and as she felt her orgasm peak she felt Ben's release too. Complete and fulfilled.

They collapsed in each other's arms, spent and satisfied.

She was nestled against his chest now, wrapped in his arms, slight and warm, a perfect fit. Her eyes were closed and he could feel her body relax against him, smell the fresh scent of orange blossom that he knew would forever remind him of her. He ducked his head and kissed her eyelids and was surprised to find they tasted salty. He looked more closely, studying her face in the faint light. There were tears on her cheeks.

'Oh, God, Maggie, what's wrong? Did I hurt you?'

She shook her head and smiled.

'You're all right?'

She nodded. 'I'm great. In fact, I haven't felt this good in years.'

'But you're crying.' He brushed a strand of hair from her cheek, surprised to see her smiling up at him.

'Don't worry, they're happy tears. Tears of release, I think. I'd forgotten how great good sex feels.'

Ben prided himself on his understanding of women. He thought he was usually pretty attuned to their desires and needs but tears were the one thing he'd never managed to master. Happy tears were a bizarre concept to him but he was prepared to believe her. She certainly looked happy enough.

'In that case,' he said, choosing to take her at her word, 'shall we move to the bedroom and try it again? Make sure it gets imprinted on your memory this time so you don't forget too easily.'

Maggie followed him to his room and they made love again in his bed, taking their time, exploring each other and finding their rhythm. Ben revelled in Maggie's lack of self-conscious-ness. He was used to women finding fault with their own bodies and over the years he'd come to find ways of praising them and making them feel good about themselves, but Maggie ac-cepted her body—other than the bump in her nose, he thought with a smile—and she was happy to share it with him. Her confidence was both enticing and illuminating.

Eventually they fell asleep, completely ex-hausted and completely relaxed. She was wrapped in Ben's embrace, and they barely moved until the morning sun disturbed them, hours later.

He woke first and lay still, waiting for the familiar flutter of panic that always came the first time he woke up with a new woman in his bed. There was always a moment when he wondered what he would say and how he would feel. Sometimes the women talked enough for them both, sometimes they continued on from the night before, having no need for words, and sometimes things were awkward, stilted, forced. He lifted his head to watch Maggie as she lay sleeping and knew things would be OK. He wanted her to be there. She looked good in his bed; she looked calm and peaceful and there was no need to disturb her.

He was able to breathe deeply. His breaths came easily; panic wasn't squeezing his lungs. He covered Maggie with the sheet as he slid out of bed. He'd let her sleep while he kept his promise from last night.

She was still sleeping when he returned from the kitchen but she stirred as he sat on the edge of the bed. She opened her eyes and her pupils shrank in the light and contrasted with the brilliant blue of her irises.

He leant forwards, kissing her. 'Good morning. Did you sleep well?'

She smiled. 'Morning. I slept like a baby. No, I slept better than a baby.'

'Are you hungry?'

'Starving.'

'I made you toast, with Vegemite, as promised.'

Maggie rolled onto her side and grinned up at him as she reached for the plate in his lap and pinched a slice. 'You're a star,' she said as she bit into the toast.

'I don't know about that but I like to think I'm a man of my word.'

Maggie sat up and moved across to the other side of the bed. 'Are you hopping back in?' The sheet had fallen to her waist but she made no effort to pull it back up to cover her nakedness. She lay back on the pillows, eating toast and looking completely relaxed. He didn't need to be asked twice. They lay in his bed, both completely naked, and ate toast while they talked.

The next two weeks were some of the happiest of Maggie's life.

She and Juliet had a routine worked out and the kids were settled. Edward's wound had healed and he was back at the football clinics, a bit of a local hero with the remnants of his black eyes. Maggie and Ben took the boys to football as it was precious time they could spend together, and a couple of nights a week Maggie would sneak out, once she'd helped

Juliet with the kids, and have dinner or see a movie with Ben or just spend the evening at his place, in his bed.

At the end of the two weeks Maggie's daughter, Sophie, had flown down to Melbourne for the weekend to watch Kate's ballet recital. Despite knowing she'd miss him terribly, even if it was only for a couple of days, Maggie had given Ben a leave pass. She hadn't expected him to meet her daughter but he'd insisted and he'd charmed Sophie, just as he'd charmed her.

Maggie was happy and content. She knew this time with Ben wasn't going to last forever. In fact, the end was near as he was leaving for Uganda in seven days, but while she didn't want to think about her life post-Ben she did feel as though she'd be able to tackle any challenges that came her way. She felt strong.

And at times she also felt as though there were two of her. The responsible Maggie—the mother, the sister, the aunt—and the Maggie that appeared when she was alone with Ben. The fun Maggie.

She'd found herself again. Ben's company was good for her.

Ben was good for her.

But she was realistic enough to know this situation couldn't last forever. Realistic enough to know his departure for Uganda would be their conclusion. They were two people, meeting by chance, who happened to form a strong connection but one that would almost certainly be broken once circumstances changed, once geography came into play. It was ridiculous to think this could last any longer than the next few days so Maggie was going to enjoy it until then.

CHAPTER SEVEN

FOUR days to go. Just enough time to still be counting in days but not enough time to ignore the fact Ben would soon be gone.

Juliet was in hospital again. Ben had done the breast reconstruction and, fortunately, with this surgery, there had been no dramas, but it did mean that Maggie's routine underwent some minor adjustments. Her time wasn't quite so free now as she became the primary carer for Juliet's children again.

Her time was divided between the hospital, the school, the children's extra-curricular activities, the supermarket and the house. If she was lucky and everything went according to the new plan she might be able to spend some time with Ben over the weekend but that was still two days away.

Maggie was leaving Juliet's room after her morning visit as Ben came down the hospital corridor. The unexpected meeting instantly set her pulse racing.

'Hey, there.' He grinned broadly at her, his blue eyes shining. 'I was hoping I'd run into you. Have you got a second? There's something I need to ask you.' He opened the door of the room opposite Juliet's.

Maggie frowned as he pulled her inside, closing the door behind them. The room was empty. 'How did you know this room wasn't being used?'

'I have my sources.' He winked at her as he pulled her in close and kissed her hard. Maggie didn't resist. She'd learnt over the past three weeks that her resistance when it came to Ben McMahon was fairly pathetic. 'Have you got time to see me over the weekend? I leave for Africa in four days.'

Maggie couldn't resist teasing him just a little. 'Juliet tells me you're planning on discharging her tomorrow.' She raised an eyebrow in question—Ben knew she'd be needed to look after Juliet and her kids.

'Damn. I guess you'll be busy. I didn't plan that very well.'

He looked genuinely disappointed and Maggie took pity. 'Actually, Juliet's ex-husband is coming to town to help with the kids. He's got shore leave so I should have some free time once we all get sorted. He gets in tonight.'

'You're kidding? You can spend the whole weekend with me?'

That had been part of Maggie's plan. 'Most of it, I hope, depending on how Sam goes.' She grinned at Ben. 'Once Sam and I get Juliet home and settled, I'm all yours.'

'Fantastic.' Ben stepped forward, moving Maggie backwards a pace or two, and she felt the edge of a hospital bed behind her thighs. Ben reached behind him and pulled the privacy curtain around the bed, screening them from the small window in the door. He bent his head down and kissed her again. She leant backwards and her top pulled away from her jeans. She felt Ben's hand slip underneath her shirt, warm against her waist, and she held her breath as his hand rose higher. 'It's a pity these doors don't have locks on them,' he said as his thumb teased her nipple, sending a wave of desire through her.

'You'd better make sure you pack tonight. You won't have time to do that on the weekend,' she said before kissing him back. She couldn't believe how wanton she'd become. Ben had reignited her libido, and she'd embraced it wholeheartedly. 'But you'd better get back to work before someone comes looking for you.' It took all her strength to resist the sensations exploding through her, to resist him, but somehow she managed it. 'I'll see you on Saturday. I'll get away as soon as I can.' She kissed him again, quickly, before pushing him out the door. She gave herself a few moments to straighten her clothing before she followed, floating on a cushion of excitement and expectation as she thought ahead to the weekend.

Ben had been pacing backwards and forwards between his kitchen and living room for the best part of an hour. Maggie had hoped she'd be able to get away from Juliet's house after lunch, and even though she hadn't been specific he'd been restless ever since the clock had struck two.

This was completely out of character for him.

To plan to spend a weekend with someone was not his normal style. That wasn't to say he hadn't done it—it had happened often but he'd never planned it in advance. He'd never wanted to make a habit of spending that much time with one woman and he definitely never extended an invitation in advance.

Yet here he was, keeping a vigil near the front door, waiting for the bell to chime. Waiting for this moment.

The doorbell buzzed and he made himself count to ten before opening the door, testing his self-control.

She was holding a small overnight bag. She was here to stay. He waited for the familiar feeling of panic to hit his chest. But nothing happened. Knowing Maggie was going to be in his house, in his bed, for the weekend didn't scare him at all. He had to admit he was quite excited by the prospect.

He took her bag from her hand and dropped it in the hallway before pulling her inside and closing the door. He knew their time together was running out fast now, and it took enormous restraint just to get them to the bedroom before he undressed her.

At six o'clock Maggie's stomach began to grumble. She put her hand over it in an attempt to dampen the noise but the sound was unmistakable and made them both laugh. They'd spent the whole afternoon in bed and food had been the last thing on their minds.

'The fridge is almost empty,' he said. He hadn't bothered to go shopping, knowing he was leaving for Africa on Monday. 'We'll have to go out to eat or get takeaway. What do you feel like? Italian, Asian, Greek, seafood? Any preference?'

'Can we go to Bella's again?'

He hesitated; Maggie was only the second woman he'd ever taken to Bella's; normally he went on his own or with Gabby, Finn and Rory. He told himself it was a chance to catch up with family, and he included Isabella and Marco in that collective. In reality, it was because the one time he'd taken a girlfriend Isabella had told him off. She'd said, in no uncertain terms, that neither she nor Marco were interested in meeting everyone he dated and unless he was serious about the girl he shouldn't bring her to their restaurant. And he hadn't. Until Maggie. And now she wanted to go again.

The look on Marco's face as Ben arrived with Maggie was enough to have him squirming. Isabella had looked like the cat who'd gotten the cream, and Ben wasn't brave enough to deny their satisfied grins. He wasn't brave enough to put a label on his feelings. Not for himself and definitely not for anyone else.

He ignored the questions in their expressions and quietly took the table they offered. He decided he could last another couple of days, and then he wouldn't have to think about this relationship with Maggie and what it meant to him. He'd be on the other side of the world. Safely on the other side of the world.

But knowing their time together was going to come to a natural end wasn't filling him with the usual sense of anticipation. Normally he'd be ready for the next adventure, the next woman, but he found himself almost regretting the fact he was bound for Uganda. Almost wanting to delay the inevitable. Almost.

'Thirty-six hours left,' he said as he polished off the remains of his lasagne.

'Thirty-five,' Maggie said with a smile.

He tried to smile back but it felt forced. How could this be? 'Thirty-five,' he agreed.

'How should we spend our final hours?' Maggie asked.

'Are they?' Hearing her description he realised he wasn't ready for the end.

Maggie frowned. 'Are they what?'

'Our final hours.'

'We come from—' she paused, seeming to collect her thoughts '—not two different worlds exactly but two different places. It's impossible to think we can have more than this.'

'Plenty of people have long-distance relationships—it's not uncommon,' he said.

'No, but it's silly. I understand that sometimes people do it because they have to. One partner has to go away for work, that sort of thing, but ultimately people have to live in the same place for it to succeed. Most long-distance relationships fail.' She reached across the table and took his hand. He felt her trying to soften her blows but they continued to land on him, pummelling his heart. 'You have your life, I have mine. There were never any promises. I don't deny it will be hard to say goodbye but we always knew this would come to an end.'

'It doesn't have to.'

She didn't answer immediately. He thought she was thinking things over. It turned out she was looking for a way to let him down gently. 'Don't feel you owe me a commitment. I'm a big girl. I've been on my own before.'

Her words were like a knife through his gut. He hadn't expected her to be prepared to walk away like this. He had to give it another shot. 'I know but I'd like to see you again—when I get home.' He could scarcely believe these words were spilling from his lips. He never pleaded, yet here he was, almost begging someone to wait for him, to see him again.

He put his wine glass down; perhaps he'd better stick to water.

She shook her head. 'I'm not the one you're looking for. I've been married, I've had my kids. You've got all that ahead of you.'

'I don't want to do those things.'

'One day you'll understand. You're almost

forty. There will come a time when you wonder what you've been working so hard for, what the point of your life is. You'll fall in love with a girl—she'll probably be very different from all your past girlfriends and probably ten years younger than you—and you'll want to marry her. You'll want her to be the mother of your children. And you should. You'd be a terrific father. You'd be surprised how happy you could be.'

I'm happy now, he wanted to say. But the words got stuck in his throat.

'Please, let's not make any promises tonight. I would like to see you again but there's nothing worse than promises that can't be kept, and this way we have no expectations,' she said.

She was giving him an escape clause, making it easy for him.

He didn't want her to make it easy. He didn't want to listen.

She smiled at him, a smile that left no doubt in his mind about where her thoughts lay. 'Why don't we skip dessert and make the most of the few hours we have left?'

Knowing she wasn't completely immune

to his charms soothed his wounded ego. She didn't need to ask him twice. He paid Marco and tried to ignore his friend's perceptive glances.

He thought he'd try to have the conversation again when they got home but Maggie had other ideas.

'No more talking,' she said. She slid his jacket from his shoulders. 'We've got thirty-three hours left—' she undid the buttons on his shirt '—and I've got plans for you. I hope you took my advice and packed already.' One by one she slipped the buttons through the buttonholes until she could lay her hands on his bare chest. She ran one thumb over his nipple, caressing it until it hardened. 'My plans don't involve talking or watching you pack and I'll warn you now,' she said as she ran her hand down his stomach and loosened his belt, 'you might not get time to sleep either.'

He closed his eyes as her hand travelled lower. He focused on the pressure of her fingers on his skin, lost in the shivers he felt flowing through his body. He heard her whisper, 'You can sleep on the plane.'

He opened his eyes. Her gaze was unwavering and he watched, entranced, as she parted her lips and licked them with the tip of her tongue.

He groaned, giving in to his desire, giving in to hers. He wrapped one arm around her back, buried his other hand in her hair and pulled her to him, kissing her hard.

She was dangerous. He couldn't afford to lose control, he knew that, but this was too much. He couldn't resist her, couldn't fight it. He was only a man. A powerless man. The world ceased to exist except for Maggie.

Nothing else mattered.

There *was* nothing else.

He felt her move her hand on his chest, felt it brush over one nipple. Felt a rush of blood to his groin. He breathed her name and that was the last coherent thought he had. With one arm he scooped her up, holding her against his chest, pressing her to him. He turned, pinning her back to the wall, searching for her mouth. He felt her legs wrap around his waist, pinning him to her. Her hands were in his hair. He had one hand around her back, the other pressed hard against the wall, afraid if he let go his legs wouldn't have the strength to support them.

Then Maggie pushed her hips against his and his resistance crumbled. She pushed him back a step, unwrapping herself from his waist, and pulled him by the hand to his room. He followed—what else could he do?

In silence, she pushed him onto his bed. They had no need for words; she had successfully eradicated all thoughts of conversation from his mind. He lay where she put him, powerless, as she lifted her arms to remove her top. He reached for her but she wasn't finished. She pulled his belt from its loops and undid his trousers, releasing him from their constraints before lifting her skirt and stepping out of her underwear. Only then did she let him take her hand and pull her onto his lap, her legs straddling him.

He cupped her breast in his hand, teasing the nipple with his thumb, making her moan. She leant forwards, offering herself to him, and he took one breast in his mouth, sucking hard. Maggie gasped and writhed in his arms. He felt her hand close around him, heard his own moan in reply.

There was no thought of abstinence. He only just remembered protection before she guided him into her, urgently, unable to hold back. There was nothing gentle in their lovemaking. It was fuelled by pure desire. Desperate, all-consuming desire.

They clung together, making love as though it might be the last time. Maggie rocked her hips and moved lower, pressing her bottom into his groin as she slid him into her warmth before she rose up again, exposing the length of his shaft to the air, then lowering herself once more to take him inside her. Up and down she moved, faster and faster, until she brought him undone and they climaxed together.

Completely spent he gathered her to him, holding her close, reluctant to let her go. He held her as their heart rates slowed and their breathing returned to normal. He wanted to savour this moment. Who knew what their future held? Each moment had to be appreciated. Each moment deserved to be enjoyed.

He lay there and listened to the sound of her

breathing, enjoying the weight of her as she lay across his chest. Her hair was fanned out and he could smell the faint trace of orange blossom, the scent of her shampoo, the scent he'd come to associate with her. He wasn't ready to say goodbye; he wasn't ready to give her up, but what other option did he have? She was right, long-distance relationships invariably failed.

They'd made no promises and they'd embarked on this affair knowing their time was finite. Could he offer more than a continuing long-distance affair?

He knew he wouldn't. As much as he wanted to he wasn't brave enough to take that step. He would leave for Africa and she would return to Sydney. He would have to let her go.

He felt her breath as it brushed his chest, and it was almost enough to bring him undone, almost enough to make him try one last time, almost enough to make him beg her for one last chance. Almost.

But when he boarded his flight to Entebbe International Airport via Sydney and Johannesburg the status quo remained. He and Maggie had gone their separate ways, and all he had to take comfort in was a vague promise that they would see how they felt when he returned in eight weeks.

Bidding goodbye to Maggie had taken the gloss off returning to Africa. He'd never felt less like leaving.

The two weeks since Ben had left couldn't have felt more different to Maggie than the weeks they'd shared prior to his departure. Saying goodbye had been one of the hardest things she'd ever done but she hadn't been able to see any other option. She couldn't see how they would make the relationship work when they lived nearly a thousand kilometres apart and she wasn't sure that they even wanted the same things.

She didn't even know what *she* wanted any more, and it was easier to walk away sooner rather than later, before she got in much deeper. She didn't think she'd find it so easy if they continued.

One of them had to be strong. It had to be her.

Maggie had returned to Sydney but she'd

come home with a gastro bug that was proving difficult to shake off. She was listless and drained and lacked her usual energy and spark. It was as though Ben had taken that with him when he left.

She was back at work but when she got home at the end of a shift she collapsed onto the couch, exhausted. Her children were virtually fending for themselves, and although they were adults and the three of them usually shared household chores Maggie normally did most of the grocery shopping and cooking. She was feeling guilty about her lack of contribution but the thought of shopping and cooking made her stomach churn, thanks to the gastro bug.

She was resting on the couch when the phone rang. She always found enough energy to answer just in case it was Ben. The phone lines weren't that reliable in Uganda, and Maggie didn't want to miss an opportunity to talk to him. He'd rung her a few times and even though they usually had to talk over some dreadful static and cope with the line dropping out Maggie knew that some form of conversation was better than nothing at all.

This time though the call was from Juliet.

'Hi, Mags. Sorry, did I wake you?'

'I was just having a catnap. I'm still so tired from this gastro thing.'

'You're still not better?'

'Not a hundred per cent.'

'Are you eating again?'

'No, I can't stand the thought of eating yet. Toast is about as much as I can handle.'

'Tired, no appetite—two weeks is a long time to take to get over a gastro bug. Are you sure it's not something else?' Juliet asked.

'Like what?'

'Menopause.'

Maggie felt her eyes widen at the thought. 'You're kidding, aren't you?'

'You've got some of the symptoms.'

'I have not!'

'Well, either that or you're pregnant.'

That made her laugh, 'God, I hope not.' Somehow that idea was more entertaining than it was horrific. 'No, no, I'm pretty sure it's not that. I'm sure I'll feel better eventually. So how are you?'

'Good. I saw Dr Clark, Ben's offsider, and he's really pleased with me.'

'And Sam? How's everything going?'

'We haven't been arguing, so that's a good start.'

Juliet sounded happy and Maggie was pleased for her. She was a naturally positive person but during the past couple of phone calls she really sounded as though she was getting her zest for life back. Maggie wondered if any of that was due to her ex-husband's presence.

They chatted for a while and after Juliet hung up Maggie pondered her sister's relationship with her ex. She was busy wondering if Juliet and Sam would try to rekindle their relationship when another wave of nausea hit her. She hadn't mentioned this continuing nausea to her sister—there wasn't anything she could do to help when she was almost a thousand kilometres away in another city—but Maggie wondered whether Juliet could have accurately diagnosed her condition via a phone call.

She couldn't be pregnant, could she?

She tried to remember when she'd had her last period. She'd had one when Juliet was first in hospital, when she'd almost died. Had she had one since?

She must have been due again around the time Ben left for Africa—maybe the week before that? But it hadn't come. Had she missed one because she was sick or was there another reason? Had she missed a period because she was already pregnant?

Absentmindedly she pressed on her boobs. They were tender but they usually were just before her period. Maybe she'd just miscalculated. There was plenty going on; it would be understandable if she were distracted.

But her boobs were always tender when she was pregnant too.

She couldn't be, could she?

There was only one way to know for sure.

Maggie walked around to the local pharmacy and bought a home pregnancy-test kit. She couldn't believe she was doing this. Walking home she felt as though everyone she passed could see through the paper bag, see the test kit she carried, and she was sure they all thought,

Foolish old woman, what do you think you're doing?

Nearing home her steps got slower and slower as she approached her front door. She was terrified of doing the test. What if it was positive? What would she do, a forty-two-year-old single mother with an already grown family? She couldn't go back to those days.

She sat on her bed, staring at the box and reading the instructions at least five times. Most of it didn't sink in but she already knew the basics. Wee on the stick, wait ten minutes and check the results. One pink line would show the test was working but that would be all—everything normal, no pregnancy, no reason to panic.

Two pink lines would mean trouble.

Eventually she summoned up enough courage to go to the bathroom but then stage fright set in. The instructions said to wee on the stick mid-stream. How did the manufacturers expect a mature woman, who'd already had a couple of babies years ago, to be able to control her wee well enough to wee, hold, put the stick in the right place, then start to wee again? It was a recipe for disaster, in her opinion.

She tore open the packet and removed the stick. Enough procrastinating.

She managed to follow the instructions, just. Wee, stop, hold stick, wee again, then wait.

One pink line, the test was working.

How long before the second line would show up?

She checked the instructions again. Ten minutes.

She put the stick on the edge of the basin and flushed the toilet, closing the lid.

As she sat, waiting for the second line, she asked herself what she was wishing for.

Did she want to see the second line or not?

Not.

I don't want to be pregnant, do I? A single mother at the age of forty-two?

No.

She waited well past the ten minutes the instructions advised.

She closed her eyes and turned her head towards the basin, towards the stick. Slowly, hesitantly, she opened one eye and peered at the stick.

She couldn't see well enough; her vision was blurry.

She opened both eyes.

One line only. Negative.

She had her answer.

She threw the stick in the bin, a slight pang of disappointment in her chest. Would it have been so awful to be pregnant? To be carrying Ben's baby?

Maggie let her imagination run down that track, just for a moment. In a way the idea was vaguely exciting. Not as terrifying as it should be.

She pulled herself together. What was wrong with her? What was she doing contemplating pregnancy at her age?

Besides, Ben had made no secret of the fact he didn't want children, and she didn't want to do the single mother thing again—she'd had her family. No, it was just as well she wasn't pregnant.

She supposed she'd have to make a doctor's appointment now. She really wasn't feeling great, and the physical symptoms were getting a bit hard to ignore. She could pretend it was heartache but she really needed to get to the bottom of it.

It was three days before she could get an appointment with her doctor. She could have said it was an emergency but it wasn't really. She wasn't feeling any worse—she just wasn't feeling any better.

'Morning, Maggie. What can I do for you?' Dr Ebert had been Maggie's GP since her children were small. She'd seen her through some tough times after Steven's death and also when Juliet was diagnosed with breast cancer, and Maggie knew she wouldn't dismiss her symptoms as trifling. If she thought there was reason to investigate her symptoms Maggie knew she would, and if she thought there was nothing that a bit of rest wouldn't take care of, then Maggie was happy to take her advice.

Maggie took a seat and tried to describe her ailments as best she could. 'I've been feeling flat for the past three weeks but it's nothing that I can really pin down. It started with what I thought was a case of too much red wine but the next day I still felt nauseous. I had a slight temperature and I thought maybe I'd picked up a gastro bug but while I felt queasy I wasn't actually vomiting. I still feel a bit off-colour but I can't make my symptoms fit one particular box.'

'Are your symptoms getting better or worse?'

'Neither really. I'm not getting worse—I just don't feel a hundred per cent.'

'Let's start with the basics, then, shall we?' Dr Ebert said as she fastened the blood pressure cuff around Maggie's arm. 'Are you on any medication?'

'No, an occasional paracetamol.'

'Headaches?'

Maggie thought about that question for a moment. 'Not currently.'

'Are you sleeping OK?' she asked as she popped the thermometer in Maggie's ear.

'I'm really tired. I think I'm asleep before my head hits the pillow and I wake up during the night to go to the loo but I can usually go back to sleep. No different to normal, I don't think.'

'You're not going to the toilet more often than

normal?' asked the doctor. 'Your BP is fine but your temperature is a bit raised. You don't think you could have a UTI?'

Maggie shook her head. 'I might be going to the toilet a little more frequently but there's no discomfort.'

'How are your children and the rest of your family?' Dr Ebert asked as she checked the glands in Maggie's neck. 'Are they all well?'

'Pretty good. I've just been down to Melbourne to stay with Juliet while she had her breast reconstruction surgery.'

'How did that go?'

'Good. She had a few dramas initially but she's managing well now and her ex is in town for a while too, giving her a hand.'

'What sort of dramas?'

'She had a reaction to the anaesthetic when she was having the expanders put in initially. She had to be resuscitated but there were no after-effects.'

'And you're OK with that? You don't feel stressed at all?'

'No, I know what I'm like when I'm stressed—this isn't it.' Lonely maybe, she thought, but loneliness didn't manifest as physical symptoms, did it?

'I think I'd better run some blood tests, see if that shows anything. Check your hormone levels. You haven't experienced any hot flushes?'

'I feel slightly feverish but that's fairly constant, nothing I'd actually call a hot flush—no night sweats or palpitations.'

Dr Ebert tightened the tourniquet around Maggie's upper arm. 'Squeeze your fist for me.' She slid a needle into Maggie's vein and filled some small vials with blood as she continued her questioning. 'Do you know how old your mother was when she went through menopause?'

'Not you too?' Maggie moaned. 'Juliet suggested that. She said I was either menopausal or pregnant.'

'Is there a chance you could be pregnant?' Dr Ebert capped the last test tube and released the tourniquet as Maggie put pressure over the puncture site.

'I guess so. Technically. But I did a pregnancy test last week and it was negative.'

'When was your last period?

'Six weeks ago.' Maggie had actually sat down and calculated it properly before coming to this appointment.

'Let's do another test just in case.' Dr Ebert took the cotton-wool ball from Maggie and taped over the puncture wound in her elbow before handing her a specimen jar. 'Can you go out to the bathroom and bring me back a sample?' Maggie pulled a face; she hated these little jars. Dr Ebert saw her expression and added, 'There has to be some reason for your symptoms. You've got to admit, pregnancy fits.'

'Surely there are other possibilities?'

'Yes, some less than desirable ones like ovarian cancer. What would you rather choose?'

'A nasty gastro virus, which is what I thought this was,' Maggie sulked.

'We'll eliminate the options one by one, shall we? Starting with the easy ones. Off you go.' Dr Ebert smiled and waved her out the door.

Maggie did as she was told and handed back the jar on her return, waiting nervously as Dr Ebert tested the sample.

'You said you couldn't make your symptoms fit any one box. I think that's because you stopped looking too soon.'

Maggie frowned. 'What are you saying?'

'I'm saying this test is positive. Congratulations! You're pregnant.'

CHAPTER EIGHT

'WHAT?' Maggie stared at her doctor.

'You're pregnant.'

Maggie rubbed her face as the diagnosis sunk in. She covered her mouth with her hands and she took a deep breath. She really wasn't prepared for this news and she'd bet Ben wasn't either.

Dr Ebert ran through some more details with her, and by the time Maggie walked out of the medical clinic her head was spinning. No more hypotheticals; she really was pregnant. She had the test result and the referral letter to her obstetrician in her handbag to prove it.

She needed to let Ben know. She felt nauseous and she knew that feeling couldn't be blamed on the pregnancy this time. It was purely and simply nervousness.

He knew she was going to the doctor today; she'd told him that much during their last phone call. Would he ring to find out what had happened?

What would he say?

She knew all too well his thoughts on fatherhood. But when confronted with the probability instead of the possibility would he change his opinion?

She checked her watch. Uganda was seven hours behind Sydney so that made it only four in the morning there. Even if he managed to ring her today it wouldn't be for a few hours. She had at least three hours to get through, and spending that time trying to imagine what his reaction would be would do her head in. She needed to find another distraction.

Maggie went home via the bookstore. Her last experience of pregnancy was almost twenty years ago and she thought, hoped, antenatal care would have changed since then, particularly as she was now, according to Dr Ebert, going to experience a 'geriatric' pregnancy. Dr Ebert had been teasing but Maggie didn't find it that amusing. She hoped reading would help pass the time, help to keep her mind occupied and focused on something other than Ben's reaction.

She wondered if there were books that were written specifically for 'geriatric' mothers. She perused the bookshelves and found a couple. She bought one, figuring she might as well be properly informed, and left the store.

Early morning was Ben's favourite time of the day in Kampala, before the humidity and temperature made conditions hot, sticky and uncomfortable. The air smelt clean and fresh just after sunrise and the traffic hadn't yet polluted the city. The Ugandan capital was a lush, vibrant place, surrounded by hills and with numerous parks and gardens—plants flourished in the tropical conditions.

Ben preferred to walk to the hospital, and most mornings he wandered through the food market near the hotel to buy his breakfast. He usually purchased local Ugandan produce, banana or pawpaw, but today the scent of oranges was heavy in the air. The smell was irresistible, instantly reminding him of Maggie and the fragrance of her hair.

He was missing her, more than he'd expected to. He missed the smoothness of her skin, the taste of her lips and the way she laughed—she laughed like someone who really meant to and her laugh was infectious. He missed the freckles scattered over the bump in her nose and he missed the way she ate Vegemite toast when he made it for her, as if she hadn't eaten in a week. She said it tasted better when someone else made it, and breakfast in bed, made by him, had become their morning ritual. He missed seeing her smile but most of all he missed her fragrance, the fresh orange-blossom scent of her.

He stood in the middle of the market surrounded by memories. Usually he found himself totally immersed in Africa—it was all-consuming and there was usually no room in his head for thoughts of home—but the memories kept coming, forcing their way into his consciousness. It was a strange experience, to have his two worlds collide like this.

He paid for the oranges, holding them up to his nose and inhaling deeply, thinking about

Maggie. He could almost picture her here, wide-eyed and fascinated.

He remembered she had a doctor's appointment today. It was unusual for someone who was normally fit and healthy to have a virus that dragged on this long, and he hoped that a virus was all that was wrong. He started walking—he'd call her as soon as he got to the hospital and find out how she was.

He peeled and segmented the oranges as he dialled her number. She answered on the fourth ring but an annoying echo on the line made conversation difficult. Although a clearer line wouldn't have changed anything—either way the conversation was not what he'd expected.

'Pregnant? Are you sure?'

The interference on the line must have been worse than he thought—surely he'd misheard?

'I went to the doctor today. I'm sure.'

'What about this gastro bug you thought you had?'

'Turns out it wasn't gastro.'

'Pregnant.' He tried to process the information, tried to make it fit with what he knew, but pieces were missing. 'There's no mistake?'

'No.'

'What are you going to do?' Ben felt as though he'd been winded; he could barely breathe.

'I have no idea. I'm still waiting for the news to sink in. I thought we'd work this out together.'

'Together?' The oranges, which before had tasted so sweet, turned sour in his stomach.

'Yes, I thought we could—'

'Maggie?'

Ben heard the echo of his own voice coming back along the line. *Maggie?* There was no accompanying answer. He repeated her name— still nothing. He slammed the receiver down when it was clear the line had completely dropped out and cursed under his breath. What a phone call to have from halfway around the world! He'd never felt so unable to control things.

What a bloody mess.

Pregnant!

Of all the scenarios he'd envisaged that hadn't been one of them. He'd imagined them carrying on their affair without any changes. Continuing on where they'd left off, continuing to have fun. He hadn't anticipated having to deal with a pregnancy. Not with Maggie. She'd had her family.

This was so not what he'd envisaged.

He debated about whether to try dialling her again and decided against it. He needed time to clear his mind, to get his thoughts in order. He still felt as though the wind had been knocked out of him.

Conversation could wait; it was time for damage control.

Ben gave the taxi driver the address and then put his head back and closed his eyes, hoping he could trust the cab driver to get him safely to his destination. He was exhausted.

His head snapped forwards, startling him, as the taxi stopped abruptly. He must have fallen asleep. He checked his watch, hoping the few minutes he'd had were enough to sharpen his senses that had been dulled by the long plane flight.

He paid the fare and retrieved his hand

luggage from the boot before opening the front gate and negotiating the flagstone path to the front door. It was a pleasant winter's evening but the air was chilly after the warm African temperatures he'd gotten used to over the past few weeks.

He stood by the front door, wondering if turning up unannounced was the right thing to do. He should have called from the airport—he knew that—but he'd chosen not to. He should have asked the taxi to wait while he made sure she was home.

His thought processes hadn't been that clear for the past four or five days. Since he'd last spoken to Maggie. Since she'd dropped her bombshell. He had called before leaving Uganda but hadn't managed to speak to her again.

He banged the heavy brass door knocker and heard it echo down the hallway.

He heard footsteps. Their rhythm was familiar.

The door opened.

She looked smaller than he remembered. Thinner.

'Ben!' She stepped straight into his arms.

He'd been planning on keeping his distance when he got here, physically as well as emotionally, but what could he do? Seeing her looking so small and wan and feeling her against his chest, it was a natural reflex to wrap his arms around her and hold her tight. Hugging her felt right. But it shouldn't. It couldn't. He dropped his arms and stepped back.

'What are you doing here?' He heard the excitement in her voice and hated himself for what he was going to do.

'We need to talk. And it wasn't a conversation I thought we could have over the phone, especially when we're likely to get disconnected halfway through.'

'So, what, you just flew back from Uganda?' She reached out one hand and touched him on the arm, almost as though she was checking he was really there. Her fingers were warm and soft and oddly comforting.

He lifted his arm, pretending to scratch his head but really just wanting to break the contact. No, not wanting to, needing to. He couldn't think straight when she was touching him. He nodded. 'I just landed.'

'You came straight here.' She was looking up at him, her blue eyes shining, the dusting of freckles across her nose dark against the pallor of her skin.

He shrugged and broke eye contact. 'There didn't seem much point in going anywhere else.'

She smiled. He could tell she thought his appearance was a positive thing and, coward that he was, he let her think that, for a little longer anyway. He didn't want to have this conversation on the front doorstep. He wanted to be inside, behind closed doors.

'You'd better come in,' she said as she stepped backwards, into the hall. 'Sorry, I'm so surprised I'm not thinking straight.'

He knew the feeling. Nothing was making sense. He'd been so certain of mind during the plane flight home, so sure he knew what he had to do and so sure his plan was the right one, but seeing Maggie again, feeling her touch, hearing her voice, was confusing him. He remembered how he'd missed her. Missed the softness of her skin, the smell of her hair, how the scent of oranges at the market in Kampala had reminded him of her.

He followed her down the hall. Her walk was still so familiar to him.

He remembered the plans that had been forming in his mind when he left. Plans for him and Maggie. But those plans had centred around the two of them, not around the two of them and children.

There were complications now, he reminded himself, the playing field had changed.

He followed her to the back of the house, to a living room adjacent to the kitchen. He was conscious of a sense of calm, a feeling of security, in her house but his mind was focused on things other than Maggie's living arrangements.

'Have a seat. I'll put the kettle on.'

'You haven't got anything stronger, have you?' He hated asking but he didn't think he could handle this conversation on a cup of tea, not after a twenty-four-hour trip.

'I've probably got some whiskey, would that do?' she asked from the kitchen.

'Perfect.' He was too keyed up to sit still so

he wandered around the room while he waited. The room wasn't large—there wasn't really anywhere to go—but there were plenty of photographs displayed on the bookshelf and mantelpiece. He found himself studying those but then wishing he hadn't. They were mostly of Maggie's children but there were also several family shots. He knew she was a great mother but seeing these photographs really reinforced the bond she shared with her children. And seeing the photographs didn't ease his conscience.

'Here you go.' Maggie returned and handed him a drink. 'Let's sit down.'

He deliberately chose an armchair so Maggie couldn't sit beside him and cloud his judgement. She sat on the couch at right angles to him nursing a glass of water. He studied her as he sipped his whiskey. She looked as though she'd lost weight, if that was even possible, and her normally pale complexion seemed to have an underlying touch of green.

'I imagine you've got some questions,' she said.

'You're absolutely sure you're pregnant?' He

knew, even before he saw her expression, that it probably wasn't the best opening question but it was the thing he really needed to know. It was the reason he'd flown halfway around the world. He needed to see for himself. Now he was here, looking at her, he didn't really doubt it but he still had to ask.

She frowned and a little crease appeared between her eyebrows. 'That's a strange thing to ask. Surely you wouldn't fly nearly eight thousand miles if you didn't believe me.' She paused and the crease on her forehead disappeared. 'Oh, I get it. You want proof.'

'It's not—'

She held up one hand. 'Don't.'

She stood and left the room. Now what? Should he follow her?

She returned before he'd worked out what to do. She was holding an envelope and she withdrew a piece of paper from it and handed it to him silently.

He unfolded it. A referral letter to an obstetrician. It was real.

She was pregnant. With his child.

He knew with utmost certainty that the baby was his. That part was never in doubt.

'It says here you're seven weeks.'

'Eight now.'

He frowned, trying to recall how the dates were calculated. Maggie obviously guessed he was doing sums in his head and she explained it to him.

'The first two weeks don't count. Six weeks ago we were at Gabby and Finn's art gallery.'

'Oh.' That weekend was vividly etched in his memory. His mind drifted back to the art gallery, to the picture of Maggie in her purple dress and black boots, to the taste of champagne and the orange-blossom fragrance of her hair. It was an almost perfect memory. Was that all he would have left? Memories?

'So how was Uganda?' Maggie's voice cut into his reverie. 'Did you have trouble cutting your trip short?' She was making conversation, trying to fill what she must think was an awkward silence.

'No, there're others who can hold the fort until I get back.'

'You're going back? When?'

He wondered why she sounded surprised; she knew he was supposed to be in Uganda for eight weeks. 'In a couple of days. I thought that would give us enough time to work out what we're going to do.'

Maggie frowned. 'Do?'

'Yes.' He sipped his whiskey, resisting the temptation to swallow the lot in one gulp. 'You know I don't want to be a father, and I assume you're not planning on having more children so we need to discuss our options.'

She sat back in the couch, her arms crossed in front of her, a stubborn expression on her face. 'I wasn't planning to have more children but that doesn't mean I won't.'

He finished his whiskey in one mouthful as he worked out what to say next. 'I thought you felt the same way I did about having children.'

'I wasn't planning on having more so, in theory, I suppose we did. But choosing not to have *more* children is very different to choosing not to have *any*. Unfortunately life has a way of dealing out some unexpected cards, and you don't always want the hand you get. If you're really so against being a father perhaps you'll be more careful next time.'

He'd make sure there wasn't a next time, he thought as he got up and refilled his glass from the whiskey bottle Maggie had left on the kitchen bench. This conversation was going to require more than one drink. 'I take it that means you're planning on having this baby.'

'It looks that way.'

'And what do you want from me?'

'I have no idea. I haven't thought about the logistics yet. You're not the only one who's surprised by this. What I don't understand is why you're so certain that you don't want to be a father.'

'It's a long story.'

'It may be, but I think you owe it to me to tell me.'

Did he owe her an explanation? He wasn't certain that he did. He looked at Maggie as he tried to decide what to tell her. Her expression vacillated between looking as though she was about to burst into tears and looking as though she wanted to throttle him. In the interests of everyone's safety he thought he'd better explain. 'It goes back to when I finished my residency. That was when I first planned to work in Africa. I'd decided on my specialty but I thought it would be good to get some general experience first. Africa would give me experience I couldn't get in the western world. I arranged to spend six months in Uganda after travelling for a bit.' He swirled his whiskey around, watching the way the alcohol clung to the sides of the glass. 'I was in the Greek islands when I got a message from my girlfriend telling me she was eight weeks pregnant.'

'Oh.'

He looked away from his glass and looked at Maggie, waiting to hear if she was going to elaborate on her reaction.

'My phone call was a bit like history repeating itself, wasn't it?' she said. 'What did you do?'

'I cancelled my plans for Africa and came home. I thought it was the right thing to do.'

'So, you already have a child.' Her tone was harsh, accusing. 'Have you told me the truth about anything?'

'There is no child. We lost the baby at nineteen weeks. Our relationship didn't survive.'

'Oh, Ben.'

He shrugged. He didn't want her sympathy; all he wanted was for her to understand why he wasn't going to sacrifice his dreams a second time. It was all in the past but he'd sworn never to put himself in that situation again.

'And Africa—you said last year was your first trip there?'

He nodded. 'By the time all this happened it was too late to go—I was due to start my specialty training. Studying and then establishing myself as a private specialist took years, years where I couldn't leave for extended periods of time. So I wasn't able to get away until last year. I know it sounds selfish but I've chosen to concentrate on my career and I want to be able to continue to work in Africa. I can't do that and have a family too.'

'So you sacrificed your dreams ten years ago, and now you're worried that I'm going to make you do it again?'

'I don't think you can make me but it would be the noble thing for me to do. I feel like a complete heel but the truth is, I don't want to be a father and I think I'll resent feeling like I have to do this. Like I have no choice.'

'You have a choice. We all do. Can you honestly tell me, now there's a chance you could be a father, that you don't want children at all?'

'Yes, I can. You know how many things can go wrong. Especially...' Ben bit his tongue, knowing his next words would be like a red rag to a bull.

'Especially what? Especially at my age? Is that what you were about to say?'

It seemed he'd stopped himself a fraction too late. 'You know the risks are greater with older mothers.'

'Yes, I do know that. And I've thought of that too.' She sighed. 'Look, I understand you need to know what I expect from you but I don't think I can make those decisions right now. But are you positive you don't want to be a father?'

'I don't have time for children.'

'That is ridiculous. Look at the time you spend with Rory and look at how much you enjoy that.'

'But that's on my terms.'

'And you don't think you'd enjoy your own children just as much?'

'I made a decision a long time ago to focus on my career. I can't do both.'

'Of course you can, if you want to. I know your job is important to you and I know you love Rory but all of that would pale into insignificance against your own children.'

'I've made a commitment to my career,' he said again.

'So you can commit to a job but not to a relationship?'

'We talked about our future. I was prepared to commit to seeing you when I got back from Africa. I wanted that.'

'I'm not talking about a relationship with me!' Maggie raised her voice. 'I'm talking about a relationship with your own child. I don't need you to be involved with your child for *my* sake but for their sake, and for yours. I think you should consider it.'

'I don't want to make promises I can't keep. I never thought I'd be in this position.'

'Neither did I,' she said with an exasperated

sigh. 'But we *are* in this position. And you played a part.'

'Yes, I'm aware of that and I take responsibility for that too but *you* are the one choosing to have the baby. I don't want children.'

'Fine.' Her voice was tight. 'It's obvious we're not going to resolve this tonight. Why don't we sleep on it and talk again in the morning?'

He could see the conversation going around and around in circles and he knew his fuzzy brain wouldn't cope with more discussion after the long flight. He had another sip of his whiskey and was surprised to find he'd finished the second glass, but the alcohol hadn't made him feel any better. If anything, he felt queasy. 'You're right.' He put his glass down and stood. 'I'll see you in the morning.'

'Where are you going to stay?' Maggie stood too, a frown creasing her forehead.

'I'll go to a hotel. I've been up for about twenty-four hours and I can't think straight. I probably shouldn't have come directly here. I need a shower and a sleep.'

'You're welcome to stay here.'

He should have known she'd offer. He should

have thought of this earlier. He should have checked in to a hotel first and then he wouldn't look quite so awful when he walked out.

'Thanks but I think we could both use some space.' He had to get some distance. Some perspective. Some control. He wasn't stupid. He knew he had to take some of the blame for this predicament. He hadn't been careful enough. From now on he'd show more restraint.

Maggie tossed and turned most of the night. She'd desperately wanted Ben to stay with her; she hadn't realised how badly she'd missed him. But staying with her, spending time with her, obviously wasn't on his agenda and that realisation cut her deeply.

When she'd seen him standing on her doorstep her heart had grown wings; all the worries she'd had lifted the minute she opened the door. He was back. He'd come back for her.

Or so she thought. She couldn't have misjudged the situation any more incorrectly. He hadn't even asked how she was.

She knew he'd been hit for a six with the unexpected news. She knew exactly how he felt and she knew she could easily make excuses for his behaviour, could easily justify his reaction. But she knew she shouldn't.

She'd pinned her hopes on him wanting this baby. On him wanting to be a father, but he wasn't here for her and he wasn't here for their baby. He was here to make his point. For him, nothing had changed. But everything had changed for her—she was pregnant with a baby she wanted from a man she loved.

No! She couldn't possibly love him. What a ridiculous thought. She couldn't be in love with a man who didn't want to be a father to his own child.

She turned onto her side, hugging a pillow to her chest. She was just hormonal and emotional and not thinking clearly, she told herself. She wasn't in love. She couldn't be.

Just as the birds began their morning chorus, just as she finally fell asleep, she made her decision.

She wanted this baby. With or without Ben.

When she rolled out of bed around eight, she felt awful and knew she probably looked worse. The first trimester of pregnancy never agreed with her, and she knew she looked wrung out but, today at least, she could be prepared. She showered and took some time to apply make-up. Today she could try to hide the ravages of a bad night's sleep, out-of-control hormones and morning sickness. She checked the time; he'd be here in an hour. She'd feel a lot more confident if she looked good.

Despite her pledge to do without him her heart was its usual traitorous self, leaping in her chest at the simple sight of Ben as he walked through her front door. He looked fit and tanned; just three weeks in Africa had darkened his olive complexion, giving him a healthy colour. But he still wasn't smiling and she wished, almost more than anything, to see him smile again. She thought she knew how to make that happen.

She waited until he was sitting at her kitchen table before she started talking. She didn't have time for pleasantries this morning; there was no place for them and she knew she just had to get this conversation over and done with. 'I've made a decision.' She waited until he met her eyes; she needed to have his full attention.

'I'm having the baby.' That certainly got his attention. 'If you don't want to be involved I'll respect your choice and I'll raise the baby on my own. I've been a single mother before and I know I can do it again. I don't expect anything from you.'

'Nothing? What about money?'

She shook her head. 'No, if I'm choosing to have this baby when I know you don't want it, then I don't expect you to help support it.'

'I might not want children but I can at least pay for my mistakes. Money isn't the issue.' His voice was tense; she could hear his anger.

'I realise that. But I don't want or need your money. I work now because I want to. I don't have to—Steven's life insurance has been well invested and I can support myself and the baby.'

'I'm not going to let you use another man's money to bring up my child, not when I can easily afford to do it. What sort of man do you think I am?'

I don't know any more, she thought. Her heart was heavy in her chest.

'How will you manage?'

'The same way I did last time. My children were my priority. I had to make sacrifices but I was happy to do that and I'll do it again.' Her own words pierced her heavy heart; she could feel it breaking in two. Yes, she would manage but how could she tell him she'd prefer not to? She couldn't admit how much she longed for a happy ending.

But Ben didn't argue the point and he didn't change his mind. That had been it—end of discussion. She'd given him what she thought he'd wanted—his freedom—but he still hadn't smiled. How she wished she was the type of girl who threw vases and other assorted household items. She imagined it would have been extremely satisfying to have hurled various objects at Ben as he'd walked out her door. But she kept her cool and managed not to dissolve in tears until he'd gone. Then she channelled her energy into looking after the family she already had.

CHAPTER NINE

MAGGIE's children had been out of the house all day but tonight she needed them home. She sent messages to both their mobile phones, making sure they'd be home for dinner. She needed to tell them her news before any more time passed. Despite her complaining stomach she got to work in the kitchen. At least that kept her hands busy even if her mind still had time to wander.

She wasn't surprised by Ben's decision but she was hurt and disappointed. At least he hadn't doubted that the baby was his. But it hurt that he could still be so removed from the baby and from her. Despite his explanation she still couldn't understand why he was being like this. It wasn't what she'd expected, and she was having difficulty associating this Ben with the one she'd known before she was pregnant.

Maggie watched as her children polished off the last mouthfuls of their roast dinner. She'd barely touched hers; she'd eaten some of the vegetables but she'd just pushed the meat around on her plate. It wasn't nausea that was ruining her appetite tonight, it was apprehension.

'That was terrific, Mum,' James said as he cleared the plates from the table. 'Did you make dessert?'

'Are you still hungry?' Maggie asked. James had eaten two servings of dinner but she supposed for a boy of nineteen there was always room for more food. 'There's an apple crumble in the oven.'

'Told you so,' Sophie said to her brother as he cleared the plates from the table.

'Told him what?' asked Maggie.

'Soph said that when you make sure we're going to both be home for dinner it means you've got something to tell us, especially if you make dessert,' James replied.

'Am I right?' Sophie asked. 'Is there something we need to know?'

'Do I really do that?' Maggie thought back;

she shrugged. 'Maybe you are right, because there is something I need to tell you both.'

'Oh, my God, you have cancer too,' Sophie burst out.

'What do you mean too?'

'Like Auntie Jules.'

'No, no, it's not *bad* news. I'm perfectly healthy. I'm just pregnant.'

'Pregnant!' Sophie said. 'That's worse.'

'How can that be worse?' Maggie asked. She hadn't meant to blurt it out quite so quickly but in comparison to cancer she felt the news was relatively good.

'Aren't you too old?' said James.

Maggie smiled. 'Obviously not.'

'How did that happen?' Sophie asked. She saw her mother's expression and added, 'I know *how* but what about safe sex? You've been preaching that to us for as long as I can remember.'

Maggie shrugged. 'It's not one hundred per cent foolproof, I guess.' She wondered whether she'd be struck down for lying. The first time she slept with Ben they'd gotten so carried away they hadn't even thought about protection until it was too late, but she didn't think her children needed to hear that!

'So what are you going to do? What did Ben say?' Sophie paused. 'It is Ben's, right?'

'Of course it's Ben's.' What did her children think she'd been up to? Maggie didn't want to hear the answer to that question. 'And he didn't say anything I didn't know already. He doesn't want children. He told me that almost when we first met and it seems he means it.'

'He doesn't want children?' Sophie asked. 'What does that mean exactly?'

'He doesn't want to be a father.' Maggie shrugged. 'He doesn't want to be involved.'

'What are you going to do?' James asked as he returned to the table, dessert forgotten in the oven.

'Obviously, this wasn't planned. As you so kindly pointed out I'm no spring chicken, and if you'd asked me last week, hypothetically, what I'd do I would have said it would depend a lot on the baby's father and on you two. But now it's *not* a hypothetical situation and there's only one answer—I have to have this baby. The two of you are the most important people in my life—you have been since the moment you were born—and this baby will be the same. I couldn't give it up at any stage any more than I could give either of you up.

'So, it looks like there'll be a new addition to our family. I don't expect you to be jumping for joy but I'd like to think that when you've had time to process this I can count on your support. Not with raising the baby—I don't expect that—but I think I'm going to need your support emotionally.'

Sophie stood from her chair and came around to Maggie's seat and hugged her tightly. 'Of course you have our support. You're a fabulous mum—you can do this and of course we'll be here for you.'

'Do you think Ben will change his mind?' James asked.

'I don't know. I'd like to think so but he's always made his position pretty clear.'

'When is the baby due?'

'January.'

'So there's plenty of time for him to change his mind.'

'I guess so.'

Maggie didn't tell her children she was wishing for the same thing.

Ben had been gone again for two days but she had a plan to keep him in the loop. She had no idea if it would work but she was prepared to give it her best shot. She hoped that by keeping him informed he'd start to feel part of it all and maybe change his mind about being involved.

She waited to see if he rang her once he got back to Uganda but the phone was silent. She sent her first email a few days later.

To: Ben
From: Maggie
Subject: URGENT!
Sorry to be asking but I've been reading up on all the tests that are recommended for mothers over thirty-five and the chorionic villus sampling can be done around now. It tests for chromosomal abnormalities, things like cystic fibrosis and Down's syndrome. I'm not that keen to have the test done because of associated risks but if there's any family history on your side that I

should know about could you tell me please? I'm still not sure if I would have the test, probably depends on what you say. I've attached a file explaining the test. I'm not sure how much obstetrics you remember from your med school days, probably not a lot.
Thanks.
Maggie

Ben's fingers hovered over the keyboard as he thought about his reply. He hadn't wanted to open Maggie's emails—he didn't want to be dragged into any discussion, didn't want to care—but he hadn't been able to ignore this one, not with that subject.

To: Ben
From: Maggie
Subject: Test update
Thanks for your reply. I was glad to hear there's no history on your side either 'cos it made me feel that I've made the right decision. I'm going to wait a couple of weeks and have the nuchal

translucency test instead. Much lower risk of anything going wrong and I'm only considered high risk for chromosomal defects because of my age so I'll wait.
Maggie

There was a week of silence following Maggie's last email, and Ben found himself actually wondering if anything had gone wrong. He was contemplating emailing his sister, Gabby, to see if she'd heard anything on the grapevine but he restrained himself, reminding himself he didn't want to be involved. Maggie's next email arrived later that same day.

To: Ben
From: Maggie
Subject: Ultrasound
I had an ultrasound scan today. The obstetrician was checking the baby's size against my dates. I've attached two pictures for you in case you'd like to see the baby.
Maggie

Ben deleted the email without opening the attachments, before he could be tempted to peek. He emptied the trash folder. He didn't want to see the baby; that would make it real.

Half an hour later he was still thinking about the email, wondering if he should have been so hasty.

He grabbed a cup of coffee in between consults and pulled out his wallet as he sat at his desk. Tucked inside, behind his driver's licence, was an old picture. He pulled it from its hiding place. It was an ultrasound picture. Taken ten years earlier, it was of his first child, his daughter, Angeline.

If anyone had asked him why he'd kept it all these years he probably couldn't tell them. He couldn't remember the last time he'd looked at it, yet he'd never forgotten it was there. It was the only reminder he had.

There was no grave, no birth certificate. She hadn't made it past twenty weeks so there had been no legal requirements for burial or even to name her. But of course they had named her and now that was all he had—an old photograph and a name.

He'd sacrificed everything at the time but he'd done it without a second thought. He'd done it willingly and it was only when Angeline died that he felt it had all been for nothing. So why wasn't he prepared to do it again? A child didn't ask its parents to make sacrifices but surely a child deserved that much.

Ben ran his fingers over the picture. He was getting a second chance. Should he take it— could he afford not to?

To: Ben
From: Maggie
Subject: Twelve-week update
I heard the baby's heartbeat today; it's good and strong. It was quite fast. There's some correlation between the heart rate and the sex and I'm tempted to check. The baby is starting to develop the relevant bits depending on whether it's a boy or a girl. I might be able to find out the sex when I have my eighteen-week ultrasound. Would you like to know? I'm not sure if I want to know but I have been thinking about

names. Do you want the baby to have your name? I was thinking of giving it mine so it's the same as my other children. Do you mind if it's a Petersen? Lots of questions today...sorry.
Maggie
P.S. The nuchal translucency test is scheduled for next week.

Mind? Of course I mind. Ben's immediate reaction was one of outrage. There's no way my child won't have my name. This child is a McMahon, he thought, a split second before he caught himself. He frowned and wondered when he'd started thinking of this baby as his child.

But that was the reality, wasn't it? His reality. Maggie was twelve weeks pregnant and in twenty-eight weeks she'd be having a baby, his baby. He was going to be a father, whether he liked it or not.

He leant back in his chair and rubbed his eyes. He was thirty-nine years old; he was going to father a child—a child who wouldn't know him, who wouldn't even have his name.

But he couldn't have it both ways, could he? He couldn't refuse to be involved in the child's life yet still expect Maggie to give it his name. Why would a child want its father's name in place of a father?

This child, his child, deserved better. Ben knew he was capable of being a father, a good one. He was penalising his child for something that wasn't its fault—penalising it for his mistake.

Was it too late to make amends?

His plane touched down on the international runway at Kingsford Smith Airport on a bright winter's day. His first impulse was to head straight to Maggie's but he'd learnt his lesson last time. He wasn't going to have another conversation while suffering the effects of jet lag.

He'd booked a room at the Park Hyatt in The Rocks, close to Maggie's house, and he planned to sleep off the plane flight and see Maggie tomorrow. He hoped and prayed another day wouldn't matter.

He checked in and went to bed, waking at six the next morning. It was still too early for an unexpected visit but he didn't feel like eating breakfast yet so he took a towel and swam laps in the rooftop pool as the sun rose over the harbour. He finished his laps and towelled himself dry as he watched the early-morning commuter ferries heading in to Circular Quay. It was a glorious morning, the gods were smiling, and he hoped this boded well for his day. He'd arranged for an early delivery of flowers to Maggie and had asked the florist to call him to confirm the delivery. Once he knew Maggie was home he was ready to visit.

He'd rehearsed his speech many times but his words almost failed him when he saw her. Her dark hair was pulled back into a ponytail, emphasizing her oval-shaped face. The freckles across the bridge of her nose were conspicuous today against the pale shade of her skin and her blue eyes were piercing in their intensity. They were missing their usual sparkle. Her gaze was cold and, unlike his last unexpected visit, there was no welcoming smile this time. She folded her arms across her chest in a defensive pose when she saw him at her door.

'What are you doing here?'

'I came to apologise.'

'What for?' She frowned and the familiar little crease appeared between her eyes. He wanted to reach out and smooth it away, wanted desperately to make everything all right, but he was finding it difficult to recall his well-rehearsed words.

'For my reaction to your news, our news. I realise it wasn't what you needed to hear. Or what you wanted to hear. I'm here to try to make amends. Please can I come in?' His palms were sweaty and he was aware of a feeling of disquiet. What if she didn't let him explain? He didn't have a plan B.

She let him sweat for a moment before turning and leading him into her house. As they walked past her children's bedrooms another thought occurred to him—was he going to have this conversation in front of an audience? They were another factor he hadn't considered.

'Are Sophie and James home?' he asked.

'No, it's semester break at uni. They've gone to the ski fields for a week,' she replied as she sat on the sofa.

He took the same armchair as before, facing

her. His flowers were on the mantelpiece—that was a good sign. She hadn't tossed them straight into the rubbish!

He took a deep breath and started his apology. 'There's so much I need to tell you but now I'm here I don't know what to say first. It's all important but what I really came to say was that I'm sorry. Sorry that I was halfway around the world before I realised I have an obligation, a duty, to do what's right. I want to be a part of my child's life—if you'll let me.'

'You want to be a father?'

'Yes.' He was sitting on the edge of his chair, leaning forward, his hands clasped between his knees. 'I'm sorry for the things I said. I have no excuse except to say I wasn't thinking clearly and I'd spent so many years telling myself I wasn't going to have children that my first reaction was *how did this happen*? It wasn't part of my plan and I reacted badly.'

Badly! That was an understatement but she wasn't about to debate that point with him now. There were too many other things being said. 'I don't understand what's changed?'

'I've been doing some soul searching. I gave

up all my plans ten years ago when I was expecting to be a father. No one asked me to—I did it because it was right. But when it turned out differently to what I'd expected I threw myself into my work, deciding to revive my dreams.' He stood and started pacing the floor. 'I realise now my initial reaction was purely selfish and I'm ashamed of that—it's not how I like to think of myself. Avoiding my responsibilities isn't right and it's not fair on my child. I think I could be a good father and I'd like to try.'

'What about Africa?'

'It will always be there. I might get back in a year—it might be ten, there's no way of knowing but that's OK. My priority now is the baby.'

'You're not leaving again in a couple of days?'

'No. I was thinking you might need me here. I'd like to come with you to the nuchal translucency test. It's tomorrow, isn't it?'

Maggie nodded, pleased he'd been reading her emails and paying some attention. 'Can I think about it?' she asked. She knew what her answer would be but she wasn't planning on capitulating immediately. It was his turn to wait.

Maggie was perched on the edge of the seat. She could feel the waistband of her jeans digging into her stomach and, while that was uncomfortable, she was too keyed up to sit back in the chair and relax. She'd left the waistband button undone—at thirteen weeks she couldn't fasten it any more—but perhaps she should have left the zip undone as well. She was aware she was jiggling her legs, unable to sit still.

Ben reached across from his chair and held her hand, his touch settling and unsettling her at the same time. 'Are you cold?'

'No, I need to go to the toilet!' She'd spent the morning drinking copious amounts of water, filling her bladder in preparation for the ultrasound. She did need to go to the loo but that wasn't why she was fidgeting. She'd been unexpectedly nervous today, and sitting, waiting for the diagnostic ultrasound, was giving her too much time to think. She couldn't explain her nervousness. It was easier to blame her restlessness on a full bladder.

'It should be our turn next—it'll soon be over.' Ben let go of her hand and returned to reading the newspaper.

Maggie didn't feel like talking but she was still annoyed that Ben wasn't making more of an effort. She was being unfair, she knew, because every time he'd tried to talk to her today she'd just about bitten his head off. She was nervous but she wasn't sure if she was worrying about the test or worrying about Ben. He'd talked about being a father in terms of obligation and duty—she had no doubt he'd do the right thing by her and the baby—but was that enough? She knew she wanted more; she wanted the fairy tale. Was she asking for trouble, for heartache and disappointment?

Should she settle for whatever he could give her or continue to hope that he might actually fall in love with the baby? And with her?

'Ms Petersen? You can come through now.' The technician's voice interrupted her thoughts and as she was whisked away to get undressed her nervousness increased. She got changed as quickly as possible—she needed company; being alone wasn't helping her nerves.

Maggie had changed into a hospital gown and was lying on the examination table. She had a sheet over her legs but the gown had been lifted up to expose her abdomen. Her skin was pale, her stomach only slightly rounded.

Ben was standing beside Maggie's head, trying to stay out of the way while still making sure he could see the screen on the opposite side of the bed, the screen where the image of his child would be displayed.

The radiographer, Jade, was fiddling with equipment and getting things set up. She looked about twenty years younger than him. Surely she wasn't in charge of the test? Ben was tempted to ask to see her qualifications.

'So, Maggie, Ben, you're a nurse and a doctor, is that right?'

'Yes.'

'Are you both familiar with ultrasound pictures?'

He assumed Maggie knew more about all the

various tests and procedures than he did. He was quite prepared to admit his ignorance so he answered the radiographer. 'I'm a plastic surgeon and I must admit I didn't pay a lot of attention in obstetrics. Let's pretend I'm just like all the other fathers who come in here—I know nothing!'

'Is this your first baby?'

He hesitated very slightly. 'Yes.'

'OK, then, I'll tell you what you're looking at but if you're used to reading X-rays this shouldn't be too difficult. Let's give you a look at your baby. The image will come up on that screen on your left.'

Jade applied the gel and began to move the ultrasound over Maggie's stomach. Ben saw her flinch as the cold gel made contact with her skin.

'The baby's in good position,' Jade said. 'Look—' she held the transducer steady, freezing a picture on the screen '—that's your baby's profile.' She rolled a finger over a button and a little arrow appeared on the screen. She used this to point out the baby's features. 'Forehead, nose. Oh, look, he's sucking his thumb.'

Ben was awestruck. He could see the baby's fingers curled into a little fist, pressed against his mouth as he sucked on his thumb. The picture was brilliantly clear—technology had clearly advanced in the past ten years—and he could scarcely believe he was able to watch his child moving in the womb. It was the most amazing sight he'd ever witnessed. His child. A perfect little person.

He hadn't expected to feel a connection but the bond was established now. That was his child on the screen.

Jade clicked a button and handed Ben a piece of paper that popped out of the printer. It was a copy of the image of the baby's profile. He immediately thought of the other, similar picture tucked away in his wallet. He was getting a second chance. This time he'd get it right.

The technician moved the transducer and a different image appeared on the screen. Ben could see something pulsing, expanding and contracting. 'This is the baby's heart,' Jade explained. 'He's got a good strong heartbeat.'

That was twice she'd used the masculine

pronoun. Curiosity got the better of him. 'Is it
a boy?'

'No. Just a figure of speech. Do you want to
know?'

Ben looked at Maggie. They hadn't discussed
this. He remembered Maggie mentioning it in
one of her emails but he couldn't recall whether
she'd been keen to find out or the opposite.
'What do you think? Shall we find out?'

She shook her head. 'No. I'd rather have a
surprise.'

Personally he'd had enough surprises but
he guessed it wasn't a big deal—they'd find
out sooner or later. 'OK, we'll keep some
secrets.'

'All right, then.' Jade was waiting for their
decision. 'I'll just take some measurements
to check the baby's size against your gestational dates. I'll measure the femur first—'
she moved the machine, then held it still and
clicked a button before moving it again '—and
then the biparietal diameter across the baby's
skull. How many weeks pregnant are you?'

'Thirteen.'

'OK, I'll do the nuchal translucency measurement now. That just involves measuring the fluid at the back of the baby's neck. He's in a good position so I should be able to get that done through an abdominal ultrasound without any trouble.'

Ben watched as Jade positioned the transducer twice, clicking a button each time to record the millimetres.

'Are you thirteen weeks exactly?' she asked Maggie.

'Thirteen weeks and two days.'

'OK.'

Ben watched as Jade took more measurements—was she double-checking her calculations or taking new ones?

'You're forty-two, is that right?' Jade's questions for Maggie continued.

Maggie nodded.

Jade removed the ultrasound transducer and wiped the gel from Maggie's stomach before covering her with the gown. 'I'm just going to ask the radiologist to check these measurements. I won't be long.' She flicked the machine off and the screen went blank.

Ben's heart froze in his chest. Going to get a second opinion was almost never good.

'Something's wrong, isn't it?' Maggie sat up on the bed and turned to face him. Her expression was pleading, her eyes begging him to make everything all right. 'Did you get a look at the measurement she took before she turned the machine off?'

Ben shook his head. 'No. Maybe the baby isn't in a good position after all. Maybe she needs someone with more experience. Jade looks about fifteen—she can't have been doing this for long.' Ben made excuses, saying the first things that came into his head, hoping his words would alleviate Maggie's fears. Telling her he shared her concerns wouldn't help matters.

Jade returned, bringing with her the radiologist, a softly spoken man who Ben guessed would be in his mid-forties. Jade got Maggie repositioned on the bed and repeated the ultrasound while Dr Evans watched. He nodded his head as Jade recorded the figures.

'Maggie, Ben.' Dr Evans turned to face them. 'What we're looking at is the thickness of fluid at the back of the baby's neck. More than three millimetres of fluid is considered greater than normal and puts the baby in the increased-risk category for Down's syndrome. Your measurement is three-point-five millimetres.'

Ben heard Maggie's sharp intake of breath. 'There's something wrong with our baby?' she asked.

'No, this test just suggests an increased risk—it's not conclusive. There are other factors to consider, and these include the mother's age and estimated gestational age. All these factors combine to give us a risk factor. A blood test can give us a more accurate picture. Did you have blood taken before you came here?'

Maggie nodded but Ben wondered how much of this information she was absorbing. Her response was delayed and her expression was unfocused.

'Good. Those results may take a couple of days to come back to your obstetrician but when they do you'll have more information to examine. Combining the nuchal translucency test with the blood test is about eighty-five per cent accurate but it's important to remember that this means there's a fifteen per cent chance of false-negative or false-positive results. So the scan is showing that you're of increased risk but it's not one hundred per cent accurate.'

Ben waited for Maggie to ask more questions but she was silent. He jumped into the void. 'So what do we do?'

'My recommendation is to wait for the blood results, get that information and then consider your options.'

'What are they?'

'Further testing, like an amniocentesis, or you can choose to do nothing. The test today is not definitive, it's just an indication. You need to get more information and you should have that in a day or two. Once you have more information, then you could elect to have an amniocentesis or you could choose to do nothing. Counselling can be helpful when you're trying to make a decision but I wouldn't jump to conclusions yet. Get your results and gather your facts and go from there.'

Ben wondered again how much of this information Maggie was absorbing. She hadn't said anything for several minutes now and her expression was introspective. Jade and Dr

Evans left them alone, and Maggie stood from the table and went to get changed, all without uttering a word. He suspected her silence wasn't good.

CHAPTER TEN

SHE didn't speak until he pulled out of the car park and was headed towards the city.

'Please, can we just go home? I don't feel like eating.'

'Are you sure?' He glanced over at Maggie; she looked miserable. 'It might be a good idea to keep busy.' They'd planned to go out for lunch. Maggie's appetite had returned now she was almost in the second trimester, and Ben thought they should stick to their plans.

'I'm really not in the mood to do anything and I can't see how you can be either.'

'It's only a preliminary test—it's not conclusive. You're worrying about nothing.'

'It's not nothing! There's a chance our baby could have Down's syndrome. I need to think about what that means. In my mind that takes priority over everything else. Please, just take me home.'

Maggie bent her knees and put her feet on the seat, hugging her knees to her chest. She looked defeated and Ben was worried. In his mind she was overreacting, jumping to conclusions, but he wasn't sure how to tackle the issue. He had a feeling that anything he said now would only make matters worse.

They drove home in silence.

Maggie went into the house and headed straight to her bedroom.

Ben followed her inside. She was sitting on the edge of her bed, small and vulnerable. He wasn't sure what he should do. He had a feeling she'd push him away if he tried to comfort her but he couldn't continue to stand in the middle of the room like a monolith. He felt large and cumbersome. He sat next to her, close beside her but not touching. He needed her to know he was there for her without feeling as though he was overpowering her.

'Talk to me, Maggie. I think we need to work out what's just happened. I don't think we're on the same page.'

'You were there, you heard Dr Evans. Our baby has a genetic deformity.'

'*Might* have. There's a risk, that's all.'

'But if our baby has a genetic condition, what do you want to do?'

'I'm not going to discuss hypotheticals. Let's wait until we have all the facts.'

'The blood test won't be back until tomorrow at the earliest. There's no way I can just ignore what happened until then. I'll be going through every scenario.'

'Well, make sure you include one where our baby is perfectly healthy as that is still the most likely scenario. I don't think anything will be achieved by you focusing on things that may or may not happen. If the baby has some issues we'll deal with that when we get confirmation. There's nothing we can do to change that.'

'I'm scared.'

Ben wrapped an arm around Maggie's shoulders, half-expecting her to push him away. 'All anyone wants is a healthy baby—you and I are no different to the next pregnant couple—but please don't blow today's events out of proportion. I know you're worried—that's to be expected—but don't forget the other possibilities. Whatever happens we will deal with it.' He didn't want to downplay her concerns—they were justified—but he didn't want her turning those concerns into unreasonable fear. 'Why don't you lie down and I'll bring you a cup of tea.'

'I don't want tea.'

Ben held his tongue as he tried not to take her tone personally. All he wanted was for her to be patient and wait for some more information. He supposed he should be patient in return.

She curled up on her side, her back towards him. He waited a few minutes to see if she said anything further but she continued to ignore him. Eventually he heard the change in her breathing—she'd fallen asleep, emotionally exhausted. There was a blanket lying across the foot of the bed and he draped it over her before he left the room.

He wasn't tired and he couldn't do nothing while a million thoughts ran through his mind. Maggie was hurting and he needed to find a way to fix things. He knew there was nothing he could do to change the outcome of any tests—that die had been cast—but he knew any delay in getting results was only going to compound the problem. There was nothing worse than waiting to hear bad news.

As a doctor the one thing he could do was call in favours, and he had no qualms about doing that on Maggie's behalf. He called Dr Bakewell, Maggie's obstetrician, and gave him a summary of their day before asking him to get the blood work hurried through.

He knew that an increased risk meant just that, an increased risk. It was by no means definite that there would be an abnormality. There was a much greater chance their baby would be perfectly healthy, and he hoped the blood tests would support his point of view. Seeing his child on the screen today had blown him away. He'd realised then that he didn't have to make an effort, he wanted to. His child and Maggie were more important than anything else, and there was no longer any point denying that was the way he felt. He'd made a silent promise to himself today to protect Maggie and his child but already Maggie was hurting and he was powerless. All he wanted was to give Maggie some good news.

* * *

The ringing of the telephone woke her. Her bedside clock read a quarter to five in the afternoon—she'd slept for hours! Afternoon naps always left her disoriented and Maggie lay still, putting the day's events back into order.

She remembered lying on the bed; she remembered being scared. She remembered telling Ben she was scared. He hadn't asked for more information, and she hadn't explained.

She was terrified he wouldn't want a disabled child. He'd only just come to terms with the fact he was going to be a father at all. She was scared she may end up being a single mother again and this time with a special-needs baby.

How could she have told him all that?

She was terrified he'd leave again and she couldn't bear that.

But now all she was aware of was silence. She was alone.

Where was Ben?

She sat up, pushing a blanket from her shoulders. Her bedroom door opened and he appeared. He was holding the phone and he looked drained. The day had obviously taken its toll on him too.

He sat beside her and switched on her bedside light.

'Who was that?' Maggie nodded her head at the phone.

'Juliet. She was ringing to find out how the scan went.'

Maggie took a deep breath. She should have called her sister but she hadn't gotten her head around the scan yet and wasn't ready to talk about the results. 'What did you tell her?'

'I told her about the scan but also that we're waiting for the blood test. I said you were sleeping and would call her later. Is that OK?'

She nodded. She didn't want to think about today. She wished she could forget about the scan but it was impossible. The pictures were going around and around in her head.

What if the blood test confirmed a problem? She already loved this child and she'd do anything to protect it. What terrified her now was the thought that Ben might not feel the same way. What if he didn't love this baby like she did? What then?

A wave of claustrophobia swept over her. She couldn't breathe; she needed some fresh air. She pulled on her shoes and grabbed a jacket. 'I can't stay here, I need to get out. I'm going for a walk.'

'Do you want some company?'

She didn't want to leave him but she needed some time alone. She shook her head. 'I need some space to think.'

She walked out of her house with the image of Ben standing marooned in her bedroom. While not overtly feminine it was definitely a female's room, and he looked out of place. The room didn't suit him; he didn't fit and she wondered whether he fit with her life at all. The changes he was making for her were huge, and she wondered whether it was too much to expect him to achieve. Was it just change or was it sacrifice? Was he really prepared to make the necessary sacrifices? Could she afford to believe he'd had time to make a rational decision?

She needed to believe him; she knew she wasn't strong enough to do this on her own. She loved him but she also knew that, unless he loved her too, there was no hope of a future together. He could be involved in the baby's life but she couldn't have him in her life without love.

Ben checked his watch—it was getting dark and cold, and Maggie had been gone for almost an hour. He knew, or thought he knew, what was going through her mind. He had to get her to see reason—there was no need to worry until their concerns were confirmed. It was really a waste of energy to spend time imagining *what if*, but she was obviously going through various scenarios in her head and he needed to fix this.

He needed to find her but he didn't have a clue where she might have gone. Where did she go when she was worried? He had no idea.

He couldn't wait any longer; he had to try to find her. He grabbed her car keys; he'd have to drive the streets. He didn't know what else to do.

She was walking just one block from home. Her head was down, watching the footpath, and she didn't see him approaching. He pulled up alongside her and he could see it took her a moment to register her own car, to register him behind the wheel.

'Maggie, get in, please.' He got out of the car and walked around to open her door and only then did she move. 'Are you ready to go home?' he asked once she was settled in her seat.

She shook her head.

That suited him; he knew exactly where he wanted to take her.

He drove to The Rocks and pulled up in front of the Park Hyatt. He took Maggie's hand and helped her out, handing his keys to the valet.

'Where are we going?' she asked.

'You'll see.' He led her into the lobby and crossed to the bank of elevators. He was still a guest of the hotel and neutral territory was the perfect place to have this conversation. They rode in silence to the rooftop and stepped out into the dark. The Sydney Harbour Bridge arched before them, and he heard Maggie's small intake of breath as she saw its famous shape illuminated against the night sky. It didn't matter if you'd spent your entire life in Sydney, every single view of the bridge could still take your breath away.

The air was cold but still and only a faint hum of engine noise from the evening traffic heading north over the bridge carried across to them. Ben took Maggie to the rooftop wall. He faced the harbour and turned Maggie so she stood in front of him, encircled in his arms, facing the bridge. At least she wasn't pushing him away physically; perhaps she needed the contact, perhaps she needed the comfort.

She hadn't spoken as they'd moved through the hotel, and he hoped, by letting her face the ocean and not him, she'd find it easier to tell him what was troubling her.

'Are you worried about coping with a disabled child?' he asked.

'No.' She gave the smallest shake of her head. He felt it against his chest. 'I'm scared of getting these test results.'

'What do you mean?'

'I'm scared of what will happen if the test confirms a problem. You've been so adamant that the nuchal translucency test only showed an increased risk and that everything will be fine but what if it isn't? I know I'll manage but what about you? Are you prepared to raise a child with a disability?'

'Of course I am.' He'd been watching the lights of the traffic as the cars traversed the bridge but now he looked down at Maggie. 'Why would you think otherwise?'

'You spend all your time fixing people. Making them whole and perfect. What if your child *isn't* perfect and you can't fix it?'

He'd thought she was worried about raising a child with a disability but her doubts were about him? Did she really think he would reject someone for being less than perfect?

'I don't want perfection. My job is to make a difference to people's lives. Sometimes I'm able to improve their quality of life, sometimes their self-esteem, but it's never about perfection. I'm not egotistical enough to believe I can make people perfect. I don't even know what perfect is, but I can try to make people whole. Sometimes that's physically whole and sometimes it's emotionally. Right now I'm just trying to be positive. It doesn't mean I'm going to run if the going gets tough.'

'But that's my point—you're not going to be

able to change this baby physically. Are you OK with that? Are you prepared for any eventuality?'

How did you prepare for every possible outcome? How did you prove to someone you were up to a challenge that was yet to arise?

He shrugged. 'I'm prepared for the idea that our expectations may differ from our reality but it's not my way to worry about hypothetical situations. I deal with facts, but whatever the facts are, I will be around, and together we will work everything out.' All he could do was give Maggie his word, his promise to meet any challenge.

'Even if some things are out of our control?'

'Even then.' He turned her around to face him; he needed to see her, to make sure she was listening.

'I am responsible for somebody else now—totally responsible—and whether or not our baby has a disability won't change how I feel. If our child has problems we will manage. I know we will.' He picked up Maggie's hand and held it close to his chest. 'Do you have any idea how amazing today was for me? Seeing our baby on that screen, sucking his thumb, watching his heartbeat, was a life-changing moment. To me our baby is gorgeous and always will be. This baby depends on us both, and I intend to be there for the baby and for you. No matter what issues we might face I have no intention of letting anyone down.' The wind had picked up a little and was ruffling Maggie's hair; he brushed a strand from her eyes. 'I'm here for the long haul, for the good times and bad.'

He was totally committed to her and to the baby, she had to understand that. He knelt on the terracotta terrace tiles, on one knee, still holding her hand. 'I need to do this properly.'

'No.' He looked up at Maggie. She had a horrified expression on her face, almost as if she were afraid. She was tugging his hand, trying to pull him to his feet. 'Please. Get up. Don't do this now.'

Ben held his position. 'Why not?'

'I can't.' There were tears in her blue eyes, gathering on her lashes, threatening to spill over.

He took hold of both her hands, ensuring she couldn't pull away. 'Maggie, look at me.

I'm on my knees, begging you to give me a chance. Let me prove that I'm as good as my word.'

'I can't do this now. Please. Can we do this later?'

'Talking about it later won't change the facts. We are going to raise this baby together—I'm here to stay. I'm prepared to discuss details later as long as we are agreed on those two things. OK?'

She nodded and only then did he get to his feet. Only then was he prepared to postpone the conversation. 'OK.' He'd thought that what she wanted, what she needed, was confirmation of his commitment. Maybe it was, maybe it wasn't, but at least it seemed as though she'd heard him. Maybe he'd never really understood women. He certainly couldn't understand Maggie's reasoning at times. 'I'm flying to Melbourne in the morning. Can we talk about this when I get back? Or would you rather come with me?'

'No.' She shook her head. 'I want to stay here. I want to speak to Dr Bakewell, get some information.'

'What's the hurry? Why don't you wait for all the results first?'

'I need to sort out a few things.'

'Just remember, you don't get to decide whether I'm allowed to hang around or not—that's not negotiable—I am here to stay.' He hoped she understood he wasn't going anywhere. No matter what the future held he intended to share it with her.

The airport was busy; the usual hive of weekday-morning commuter activity was all around them. Maggie held tight to Ben's hand as they negotiated the crowds, her hand at odds with her mind. They'd been existing in an uneasy truce all morning, not talking and not arguing.

She felt the burden of the nuchal translucency test weighing her down and she realised she wouldn't really be able to move on or make any reasonable decisions until she knew those results. She was sure Ben had things on his mind too. Things he wasn't disclosing to her.

She could feel the weight of their unspoken words, each word like a brick, slowly piling on top of one another, making a wall, and she wondered if that wall would ever come down. Would they be able to speak the words, take them one by one from the wall and say them out loud until the wall was gone?

She needed time to sort things through in her own mind before she'd be ready to tackle the wall.

Ben had offered to be a part of their child's life but she knew he still imagined working in Africa again one day, travelling the world. That might have been possible with an able-bodied child—would it still be possible with a disabled child? Could she expect him to give up his dreams forever? Because there was a strong possibility that's what this would mean. Would he stay or should she set him free now?

Her brain needed to get him on this flight. She couldn't think clearly when he was around and she desperately needed to think, but her hand was holding firm, her body wanting to keep him close, making the most of every minute in case she had to let him go. Each minute could be bringing them closer to the end.

She remembered his words from the night before—*you don't get to decide* whether I'm allowed to hang around or not. He was right—she couldn't make him stay and she couldn't make him leave. It was all up to him. But what he didn't understand was that she could give him permission to leave, and she still wondered if that was what he was waiting for. This was what she needed to decide today—should she give him permission to leave and how did she do that?

She walked with him to the departure lounge where they were calling his flight.

'Will you be here when I get back?' he asked.

'Of course.' Her words came easily. She didn't dare stop to think if she was speaking the truth. She hugged him tightly, wanting to savour the feel of him in case it was goodbye. She loved him; that was why this situation was impossible. If only he could love her too. 'I'm not going anywhere. I just need to get my head straight.'

He leant away from her a fraction. 'You'll be OK?'

'I'll be fine.'

'I'll see you soon.'

She stood still as he turned to board the air-craft, her arm stretching between them as he held onto her hand until it could go no further, finally letting go.

She waited as he handed the flight attendant his boarding pass and she saw the appreciative glance the attendant gave him as she processed his ticket. He turned in the doorway and she waved, staking her claim. She didn't move until he was out of sight.

She hadn't gone far when her mobile phone rang. The conversation was brief but the news had her hurrying back to the departure gate. She ran to the front of the queue, not caring that passengers were still waiting to board.

'Excuse me.' She confronted the flight attendant, the one who'd so shamelessly checked Ben out as he'd boarded. 'The man who just boarded, Dr McMahon, you have to get him off the plane.'

'Is there an emergency?'

'I need to talk to him.'

'Sorry, that's not an emergency.' The flight attendant's tone was smug and Maggie wanted to slap her.

'Please, I have to speak to him. He's right at the front, he had seat 2A. It will only take a minute.'

'I can't get him off the plane. He has checked-in luggage and he's been marked off as boarded. He doesn't come off until we get to Melbourne.'

Maggie felt her eyes narrowing and she fought to stop herself from glaring at the woman. 'Can you let me on, then?'

'Do you have a ticket?'

'You know I don't.' Maggie just managed to refrain from stamping her foot in frustration; she was ready to explode.

'I'm sorry, there's nothing I can do.'

She didn't sound sorry!

'Is there a spare seat? I'll buy a ticket.' She had to get on this plane.

'There are some seats available but the plane leaves as soon as everyone has boarded.'

One of the other flight attendants came to her aid. 'You could try the customer service desk at gate four. If you're lucky you might make it.'

'Thank you,' Maggie said as she spun on her heel and raced to the next gate lounge, dodging travellers and their bags. She bought a ticket, a horrendously expensive one, but considering seat 2B had been vacant she didn't care. Now she just prayed she wasn't too late.

She made it. She thrust her boarding pass at the smug flight attendant and ran down the air bridge and onto the plane.

Ben was already settled in his seat, reading the newspaper, and the flight attendants had begun their preflight safety talk.

She slid into her seat. 'Excuse me, is this seat taken?'

'Maggie! What are you doing here?' The look of surprise on his face was priceless. He leant across the armrest and wrapped her in a warm embrace. His reaction released her heart. The phone call had lifted a weight from her chest and now Ben's hug set her heart free. She was back where she belonged—beside him.

'I'm coming with you,' she said as she buckled her seat belt.

'To Melbourne?'

She nodded and grinned.

'What's going on?' he asked as the plane began taxiing to the runway.

'I just got a phone call from Dr Bakewell. He got the blood test results back.'

'And?'

'Everything's normal, the ultrasound was a false positive.'

'What?'

'He thinks our baby is perfectly healthy. I can have an amnio to double-check if we want to but he's confident everything is fine.'

'That's fantastic,' he said as he hugged her again. 'You got on the plane to tell me that?' She nodded. 'You know we would have managed if our child had a disability. I love our child and I love you and we would have survived.'

'You love me?' When had he decided that? And why had he waited until now to tell her? 'Why didn't you tell me?'

'It took me a while to work it out.'

'Is that why you came home?' Had he come back for her after all? Had he realised he loved her but not known how to tell her. He was shaking his head.

'I came back from Africa because I thought it was the right thing to do. I felt I owed it to our child. It deserved to have two parents. But sitting at the radiologist yesterday with you, looking at our child on the screen, I realised I wanted to be there. I want to be here for our baby and for you. I love you both—that's what I was trying to tell you last night when I was trying to propose.'

'You were?'

'Yes, but you wouldn't let me finish.'

'You never said you loved me. If you'd proposed and I'd accepted I would have always thought you'd felt trapped, forced into marrying me.'

Ben reached out for her then, taking her hands in his. She looked down, scarcely able to believe he was back, that he was holding her, that he *loved* her!

'I'm in love with the woman who is going to be the mother of my child. I think I've loved you for a long time but I've been too scared to admit it.'

'Would you try proposing again? I'll let you finish this time.'

'You're serious?'

She nodded. 'I am. You must know by now that I'm not the sort of girl who dates. I'm the sort who falls in love. And I'm in love with you. So, if you're willing to propose again, I won't interrupt.'

He laughed. 'All right, this is what *I* know.' His thumb was making tiny circles on the back of her hand, and she fought to concentrate; she didn't want to miss a word. The wall was coming down, and she was going to make sure it never came back. 'You have changed my world. You have taught me about love and commitment. Since falling in love with you I've realised some things are out of my control. There will be some things I can't fix and that's OK. It might take me a while to get my head around the idea but I will. You have shown strength and courage and altruism, and I love you more than I thought possible. Believe me when I say I'm committing to you of my own free will. I *want* to spend the rest of my life with you. Maggie Petersen, will you be my wife?'

'You're sure about this? What about your dreams—Africa, your work?'

'I thought you promised to let me finish.'

'You did finish. I'm just clarifying a few things.'

His laugh washed over her, and it was the most beautiful sound she'd ever heard. 'I was trying to hang onto my dreams instead of realising I could make new ones, with you. I have a different dream now. One where I am married to the woman I love and raising our family. One where I'm trying to be the best father I can be. And in that dream I take my family with me to Africa and to show them the world. My dream has expanded, and it's going to be better than you or I could ever imagine. So, what do you say, Maggie, will you marry me?'

He reached inside his coat and when he brought his hand out again he was holding a small box. The box was duck-egg blue. He opened the box, holding it towards her. Nestled inside was a stunning square-cut diamond set in a ring of platinum.

'You bought a ring?' It was her turn to be surprised.

'Yes, I bought a ring.'

'From Tiffany's?' Her heart was racing and

her words were tripping over themselves as they tried to keep pace with her pulse.

'Yes,' he said with a grin that had his turquoise-blue eyes sparkling.

'When?'

'Yesterday afternoon, when you were sleeping.'

'You've had it all that time?'

'Yes! For pity's sake, Maggie, would you answer the question!'

She laughed. 'Yes.' She kissed him. 'I will marry you.'

He took the ring out of the box and slid it onto her finger. It fitted perfectly. She closed her eyes as he kissed her and she could taste his promises and knew he would always be there for her.

'I love you, Maggie. I love you and I love our child.'

She knew she could believe him. She lifted her sparkling eyes to his. 'Here's to new beginnings, new dreams and new life,' she said.

Ben rested his hand on her stomach, joining the three of them together, and kissed her again.

Maggie sighed as they sealed their promise to each other with that kiss. The next stage of her life was about to begin—her world was complete and it was perfect, she couldn't ask for anything more.